PADRE: MISSION CREEP

DAVID J GATWARD

PADRE: MISSION CREEP

ISBN: 978-1-912767-18-2
Published by Zertex Media Ltd

1

www.zertexmedia.com

To Tommy ...

FOREWORD

Author's Note:

It is reported that, in January 2002, United States Marine Forces near the Tora Bora cave complex in Afghanistan experienced sonar interference on their cave mapping system. A small squad of marines was sent to investigate and destroy what was assumed to be a jamming device built by the Taliban. However, no such device was found, only one marine survived, and no rational account could ever be found to explain what he and the rest of his squad encountered down there in the darkness ...

Additional note: Operation Herrick, the codename under which all British operations in Afghanistan were conducted from the outbreak of war in 2002, came to an end on 27 October 2014. However, British forces are still on the ground in Afghanistan. Operation Toral, the codename for British presence in Afghanistan post-2014, is part of NATO's Resolute Support Mission. UK forces in

Afghanistan are now tasked with training and mentoring Afghan Forces and providing force protection for NATO advisors.

CHAPTER ONE

Afghanistan, sometime in 2017 …

FOUR MEN, all armed to the teeth, stared out from the back of the Foxhound patrol vehicle. Alex Carter, touching six foot, fit enough to run eight miles in under an hour, his skin a masterpiece of 'every scar tells a story', stared back. He'd faced off against harder. And uglier. And won. Most times, anyway. Behind him, a second Foxhound sat in the brooding heat and dust of the Afghanistan desert, the skin of the vehicle hot enough to fry an egg.

'Room for another?'

Dust was tumbling across the ground at his feet and even though it was still early in the day Alex was sweating hard, his short, black hair sticking to his skull. He wiped his forehead, waiting for an answer, trying to remember just how many times he'd been out in the badlands, not just as a soldier, but as an army padre. Not that it mattered; the thrill of being out on tour was as alive in him as ever. He could taste it in the air, feel it in his heartbeat. He belonged out here. Plus there was the fact that being out here meant he didn't have to think about Bonny too much. He missed her, but she was gone, and there was nothing he could do to bring her back. Cancer had a knack of being a full stop in too many lives, and Bonny's had been just another. Didn't make it any easier to deal with though, which is why the distraction of what he was doing right now was so welcome.

'Only got room for four,' said one of the soldiers, his face hidden in shadow, but his eyes catching light and reflecting it back out into the day with a steely glare. His voice had a snarky edge. Alex was used to it.

'Like bollocks you have,' Alex said. 'Shift it.'

A laugh barked out from inside the vehicle's armoured shell.

'You allowed to swear?' asked another of the soldiers, as they all shifted to let Alex in.

Alex climbed in and handed up what he'd been carrying to the soldier nearest the door, a man who seemed too large to have clambered inside the rear of the Foxhound in the first place. Unlike the others he was armed with a semi-automatic combat shotgun. Alex thought back to the last time he'd used one himself, some years ago now. It had done a neat job in taking off some door hinges during a raid, then gone on to work wonders in persuading the X-Rays they'd captured to give up. But then a 12-gauge, up close and personal in the face had that effect on most people.

'The fuck is this?' the soldier asked, looking at what Alex had given him.

In his hand was a length of black iron, approximately five feet long, curved at one end to form a hook, the other ending in a sharp point.

'It's a shepherd's crook,' Alex said, punting himself down between two of the other soldiers, who were all armed with SA80 automatic rifles. 'Never seen one before?'

Seeing as the rear of the Foxhound was spec'd out to seat four soldiers only, it meant that Alex didn't actually have a seat to sit on, but that didn't matter: you didn't join the army for comfort. Up front sat the driver and the officer, both of whom Alex had met only briefly before swinging round to get into the back of the vehicle.

'You know what I mean,' the soldier said.

Alex pointed at one of the SA80s, the standard issue for soldiers in the British Army. 'Weighs about the same as one of those,' he said. 'A mate didn't approve of me getting it easy by carrying less weight than a regular soldier, seeing as I'm not allowed to carry a weapon. So he had that made for me to carry instead.'

The soldier held the crook in one hand, nodding. Alex wasn't sure if it was out of approval, but he'd take that anyway. 'You carry this with you all the time?'

'Even to the bathroom,' Alex said. 'And it's a good ice breaker, right?'

'The fuck kind of ice you need to break with that?' asked the soldier on Alex's right, a young man, probably not yet even twenty. 'This is Afghan, mate, not the Arctic Circle.'

The soldier holding the crook handed it back to Alex then heaved shut the thick armour of the rear door of the Foxhound with a dull, claustrophobic clang. The thrum of the six-cylinder diesel engine grumbled through the vehicle's modular frame as the driver revved it into life.

'I'm Carter,' Alex said, introducing himself to the soldiers properly for the first time as the Foxhound thrust itself off into the day. Not that any of them could see where they were heading, sealed as they were inside a specially designed cabin with a wedge-shaped belly to deflect IED blasts, the only sky visible through the windows at the front of the vehicle. 'Only got in a few hours ago but figured it best to get out sharpish and see how things are.'

The large soldier pointed at the other soldiers in turn: 'Harper, Jackson, Fuller. I'm Northcutt. Upfront we've got Collins in the driving seat and Lieutenant Fox running this little day drip.' He leaned forward, the combat shotgun resting against his shoulder, barrel pointing up at the Foxhound's roof. 'If you don't mind me being blunt, Sir, but what the fuck is a padre doing out here anyway?'

'There somewhere better you think I should be?' Alex asked.

'Church,' said the soldier to the left of Northcutt, the one called Harper. 'Like a good little Christian.'

Alex allowed the ghost of a smile onto his face, mainly because if there was one thing he'd never got quite right about the whole being-a-padre thing, it was being a good little Christian. And he'd never really liked those who purported to be such either; most of those types he found generally needed a hard slap in the face with a bit of real life and hardship.

Northcutt jabbed Harper in the ribs hard enough to get a snarl. 'Wind your neck in, Harper,' he said.

'Sorry, Corporal,' Harper said. 'It's just that –'

'It's just nothing,' Northcutt said, cutting him short. 'For a start, padres are captains, so respect rank, you hear me?'

He then eyeballed Alex and pointed at the rest of the kit he had strapped to his yoke system. 'Padres are fully medic trained, right?' he asked.

Alex nodded. First aid wasn't all he was trained in either, but that wasn't a story for right now.

'Good enough for me,' Harper said, then he grinned and added with a wink, 'we've got God on our side, lads! What can go wrong?'

Alex smiled back but he knew his eyes weren't joining in. He didn't want to point out that the Taliban, ISIS, and every other fanatical group, from the Ku Klux Klan to The Lord's Resistance Army in Uganda, thought the same.

With that, the conversation died. Shouting to each other across the sound of the Foxhound wasn't a great way to communicate. They were all wearing personal role radios (PRRs), which worked by conducting vibrations through the skull to the inner ear, meaning you could still communicate in the thick of a fight through a chatnet, with everyone in the patrol in on the conversation. Alex knew they could've kept talking through that, but he also knew that soldiers heading off out on patrol always took a bit of quiet time to get themselves together. Routine or not, and despite the war in Afghanistan being officially over for a few years now, you still had to stay sharp.

Alex would've preferred to chat. He'd never been great at dealing with silences. And at the moment, a silence meant time to dwell on Bonny, and the fact that she wasn't around anymore. He'd be alright though, he thought. He'd lost people before. Part of the job, or at least part of the one he'd had before this.

A voice buzzed through the chatnet snapping Alex back into the moment.

'ETA fifteen,' it said, the voice of Lieutenant Fox in the front cabin sounding crisp, clear and direct through the PRR, despite the air being filled with the thrum of the Foxhound's engine, and the rumbles and knocks from the wheels navigating the terrain outside. 'Remember, we're just out here for a look-see. Area's been quiet for weeks. So let's do this nice and smooth and get back for a–'

An explosion outside the vehicle cut the conversation in half as the Foxhound bucked so hard that Alex was sent flying high to thump his head on the roof.

CHAPTER TWO

'Drive!' yelled the lieutenant from the front of the Foxhound, now hardwired into fight mode. 'Get us the fuck out of here, Collins! Now!'

Alex's helmet had saved him from a serious crack to the head but his ears were ringing like hell.

Another explosion, this one hammering into the side of the Foxhound, knocking it up onto the two wheels. It thumped back down and shockwaves jolted through Alex as the vehicle swung a hard right, the driver now focused on getting them the hell out of there and back to base.

'Fuck me, that was an RPG!' yelled Fuller.

No one disagreed: they were too busy hanging on.

The all too familiar sound of small arms fire then erupted from all around them, rounds buzzing and pinging off the Foxhound's exterior.

Alex closed his eyes briefly to calm his nerves.

'We're going to need more than a sodding prayer, Padre,' Jackson said.

Alex opened his mouth to reply but another explosion

hammered the air from his lungs as once again he was tossed into the air.

The next couple of seconds sent the world into a spin and Alex knew that whatever had just hit them had been massive, big enough to flip the Foxhound skyward and onto its roof like a toy car thrown by a toddler in a tantrum.

The truck landed hard, tipping up and forwards before rocking back to settle with its wheels helplessly spinning in the air. The reinforced windows at the front crunched and shattered, but stayed in place, still affording protection from what was going on outside.

More small arms fire rattled against the vehicle's armour-plated skin but Alex knew, as he knew they all did, that staying inside wasn't an option. Right now, though, everyone apart from Alex was still strapped in and hanging upside down.

Northcutt barked down the chatnet but there was no answer from Fox or Collins. He then turned his focus to the rest of them. 'Unclip yourselves!' he yelled, bracing himself with his hands on the roof, which was now the floor, then tumbling down to join Alex.

Alex helped the three other soldiers out of their seats.

'The fuck are we going to do now?' Fuller said. 'We go out there they'll cut us to pieces!'

As if to emphasise what the soldier had said, more small arms fire cut in, peppering the metal all around them.

'No they fucking won't, not if we do this properly,' Northcutt replied. 'You understand?'

The soldiers all nodded.

Northcutt pointed at Jackson and Alex. 'You, grab Fox and Collins. Now!'

Alex was moving before Northcutt had finished speaking. Climbing forward to the front of the upturned

Foxhound he found both the lieutenant and the driver to be unconscious. With the reinforced windshield and the glass in the doors smashed he couldn't see a thing through them but at least they gave him a little light. Rounds hammered home all around him as he did a quick check for broken necks, broken bones, then he and Jackson had both men out of their seats and in the back with the others. Cosy, Alex thought, looking up at Northcutt, who, with the lieutenant out of action, was in command. Alex knew he himself was the highest ranking officer, and also probably the most experienced soldier, but it was hardly the time or the place for a padre to pull rank, or for him to start trying to explain what he'd done before being called to be a padre. They wouldn't believe him anyway.

Northcutt pulled a couple of canisters out of one of the pouches on his webbing.

'Soon as Fuller kicks that door open,' he said, 'me and Jackson will flashbang and smoke those fuckers out. I'll take point, the rest of you follow. This is fire and manoeuvre. You know the drill, lads. Padre: you wait here with the lieutenant and Collins until you get the call from me. Ready?'

Alex saw the other soldiers nod. If they were afraid – and he knew they'd be either liars or too dangerous to be out here in the first place if they weren't – they weren't showing it. A good sign: they were well trained, experienced, and using any fear they had to give them an edge. They were all eyes on Northcutt, ready to take it to the enemy. Deep down, a part of Alex wanted to do the same: the soldier he'd shut away and locked down tight when he'd taken up his new calling. But it was noisy in there and the soldier clearly wasn't happy about not being allowed to come out to play.

'Go!'

On Northcutt's command, Fuller heaved a boot at the

rear door. As it swung open canisters went flying into the air. Everyone inside the Foxhound ducked down, hands over their ears, eyes closed. A rapid series of bangs followed by shouts from outside were the signal for Northcutt to go to war. The soldier was up and out of the Foxhound in one smooth motion, firing a few short bursts first to get the heads down of whoever had attacked them. Then Fuller, Harper and Jackson followed, same drill, same purpose in their every movement: to take it to the enemy.

It was then, as Alex waited for the call from Northcutt, that another explosion ripped the moment apart and sent it in all directions in a cloud of blood and grit and bone.

Alex was knocked back further into the Foxhound, dust choking him, his ears ringing. And when the ringing stopped all he could hear were the screams of men in agony.

Alex opened his eyes to peer out into the world beyond the upturned Foxhound and as the dust cleared he glimpsed Hell. Northcutt had stepped on an IED, one so massive it had almost cut him in half. Astonishingly, he was still alive, but only just. Around him lay Jackson, Fuller and Harper, each of them a mess from the shrapnel fragments which had torn into them. The ground was splattered with blood and bits of Northcutt. Harper was missing his left foot. Fuller's face was a mask of blood, one of his eyes gone, his left arm limp and useless. Jackson was trying to stop his guts from tumbling out of the violent rip that had torn his stomach open. And the backdrop to all of it was the burning remains of the other Foxhound, two wheels gone, on its roof, flames licking the sky. Alex knew in his gut there was no point looking for survivors.

A voice called out, hooking Alex back into the moment. He couldn't make out what it was saying at first, still deaf himself from the explosion, but when his hearing came back, the words were clear and strangely polite. 'You, still in the vehicle, come out now, please.'

Alex didn't reply. Behind him the lieutenant and the driver were coming round, but they'd be no use at all in a fight for a good while yet. Outside the rest of the squad were either close to death or soon would be if they didn't get medical attention.

'I do not want to ask you again,' the voice from outside called once more. 'Come out now. Please.'

Alex knew he was out of options. If he stayed in the vehicle, he had a horrible feeling the next thing he would see would be a grenade thrown in to keep him company. And if he went outside, then there was every chance he was going to get slotted anyway, but it was also the only thing left for him to do. He wasn't armed. Perhaps he could at least tend to the wounded? But then what? They'd all be taken hostage. And that never ended well, did it? In fact, it usually ended with a massive knife hacking your head off. Christ alive ...

Christ ...

Alex stared skywards for a moment. He had memories he'd come here to escape, had seen and done things that would rip any normal person's faith to shreds, but Alex wasn't normal. His faith had been born from moments like this, from blood. Right now, that's what he was hanging onto, a seed of something that had stopped him from going insane. But still, he prayed. Not just for himself, but for the men he was about to meet.

CHAPTER THREE

'I'M UNARMED!' ALEX CALLED OUT.

'That is for the best,' the voice replied.

'There are two men injured in here with me,' Alex said, working to keep his voice calm and measured. 'I'll come out alone.'

He didn't wait for a reply and instead, and with another quick prayer, grabbed his crook to help him get to his feet, then slowly emerged into the bright light of the day.

The stench of battle hit him on a wave of heat blasting down from above. He knew it well, but that didn't make it any the easier to bear. It wasn't just blood and sweat he could smell, but cordite from expelled rounds, explosive, smoke, burning flesh, and shit. Yeah, that was always the killer: the body didn't react well to getting torn apart; muscles would spasm, the bowels and bladder would eject whatever they contained.

Alex pulled himself up to stand, leaning against his crook to fight a sudden wave of nausea that he fought to control and only just won. He wasn't sure if it was from the concussion he'd no doubt suffered when the truck had flipped or the reek of what had happened only a few feet in front of him.

Smoke cleared and through it he saw their attackers. There were four of them but they'd done the damage of many times that number courtesy of the IEDs and the RPGs which had gone to work in the only way they could, and taken out a piece of military hardware worth close on a million Sterling. The men closed in, their weapons held at their waists, barrels facing Alex and the wounded in front of him.

'No weapons!' Alex repeated, wanting to make that absolutely clear, trying to buy time, though for what, at that moment, he hadn't a clue. Time was something none of them had and it was racing now, speeding forwards towards a conclusion he didn't want to think about.

Three of the men stopped, surrounding Alex and the fallen soldiers in front of him. The remaining man continued walking until he was in front of Alex.

'You will surrender,' he said. 'Your men are injured. There is nowhere to run to.'

The man was tall, beefy, and stank of sweat. His beard was flecked with grey and his face, hardened and deeply lined, was as kindly as a rabid dog, a scar tearing a jagged line from the base of his left eye all the way across his nose and on through his right cheek.

Alex was standing straight now, the crook relaxed in his hand, his mind alert, taking in what was around them, the lie of the land, the men. They were all armed with AK47s, large knives hung from their belts, three of them carried pistols, including the man who had spoken. The fourth was fiddling with something under the jacket he was wearing.

'I'm a trained medic,' Alex said. 'I need to –'

A fist smashed into the side of Alex's face, filling his

head with stars, causing him to stumble to his right. His foot caught against Harper's ruined leg and the man howled in agony as Alex dropped to his knees. He coughed, then saw something on the ground in front of him, something that was supposed to be in his pocket, except now it wasn't and it was covered in dust and splattered with blood. And that wasn't right because it was a photograph and there she was staring up at him, his beautiful Bonny, just a few months before the cancer had eaten her away before his eyes, and no amount of prayer, no amount of faith had been able to do anything about it and, if he was being brutally honest, that had really pissed him off. Still did.

A hand reached down and snatched the photograph up as another grabbed him behind his neck and dragged him to his feet, whipping him round to face the man with the scarred face.

'You are in no position to make demands,' the man said and, to emphasise the point, drove another fist into Alex's stomach causing him to double over, retching.

Alex coughed, fought the pain, the crook the only thing keeping him from dropping to his knees. When he stood up the man without the pistol had freed from his jacket what he'd been rummaging for and the sight of it froze Alex's blood: it was a digital camera.

'Please,' Alex said, pulling himself back to full height. 'You don't have to do this ...'

The man with the scar laughed. 'We can do whatever we want,' he said. 'But you do not need to worry: you are worth more to us alive.'

The man with the camera was now pointing it at the soldiers on the ground. He moved among them, kicking them to make them scream louder.

'But the British government doesn't negotiate with

terrorists,' Alex said, fighting to stay calm, to keep the rage, the soldier, chained up. He was a padre, a man of God, sent here because it was where he truly believed God wanted him to be. The soldier was someone he'd been long ago, someone he'd left behind. He couldn't afford to let that side of him free. Because if it did wrench itself out into the hell of right now, then ...

The man with the scar leaned in close, pulling Alex from his thoughts, the man's breath hot and laced with alcohol and the rot of teeth not cleaned for years. 'I know,' he said. 'But I have other buyers.'

Alex couldn't quite comprehend what he had just heard. 'Slaves? But we're –'

'You are nothing!' the man with the scar spat back before back-handing Alex across the face. 'You will be sold and you will be used in whatever way the buyer wishes. And when they are done with you? When your body and mind are broken and you wish for death? They will use you some more. Hell awaits you, my friend ...'

The man then brought the photograph of Bonny up in front of Alex's eyes. 'Yours?' he asked.

The man stepped back from Alex, a laugh lancing through the air as he showed the others with him the photograph.

'His dog!' he said and the others joined in, all of them laughing, like the photo of Bonny was the funniest damned thing they'd ever seen.

Alex wasn't laughing. He was fighting a battle inside between the two parts of himself, the priest holding back the trained killer with silent prayer that was becoming more and more desperate.

With no warning given, the man pulled his pistol from the holster on his belt and shot Northcutt three times in the face. The rounds smashed into the soldier, destroying his skull as only hollow points could, sending bone fragments and gore spinning into the air and across the ground. The sand became a halo of red around what remained of the skull, which wasn't much.

Alex stared in horror at the space where Northcutt's face had been barely seconds before. None of it was left. The skull was just a broken shell leaking red into the sand. It now bore more resemblance to a watermelon crushed under a boot than a human head.

The man with the scar moved his pistol from Northcutt to Fuller. The three other men were not only laughing now, they were clapping, applauding their leader for his butchery, their weapons at their sides, because they knew there was no threat from the soldiers in front of them. How could there be? One was dead, three were screaming in fear and in pain from wounds that would soon see them dead, another was unarmed, and the remaining two were injured inside the Foxhound. There was no threat here, no threat at all.

'Don't ...' Alex said, the soldier close to breaking free now, the priest inside pleading with it. 'Please ... don't ...' But the soldier was stronger, knew that if they were to get out of this, no amount of prayer was going to help, but the priest didn't want to give up, because Alex wasn't a man of violence anymore. He'd left that all behind. He'd promised.

The pistol was brought round to point at Alex.

'You are unarmed,' the man with the scar said with a laugh. 'What can you do? Nothing!'

He made to swing his aim back to the soldiers on the ground.

Alex breathed in the moment, cast a quick eye at the

men around him, clocked where they were standing, how they were standing, their weapons. 'That's not what I said.'

The man with the scar looked puzzled. 'What?'

Alex stared, his eyes cold now, wide and wild. 'I said I had no weapons. I never said I was unarmed.'

Time slowed ...

... Alex saw the man with the scar pull back the hammer of his pistol with his thumb, watched the other men ready their own weapons, saw a single black bird pass behind them on the wind, could smell them, each one of them, the rank stench of life in the desert, the sweat of soldiers, the stink of death ...

... and the soldier took over.

With a vicious and aggressive sweep upwards, Alex caught the scarred man's wrist in the hook of his cast iron crook. The pistol fired into the sky, its aim knocked away from the soldiers on the ground. Alex kept the crook moving, bringing the wrist up in a wide arc then down into the sand with such a violent wrench that the wrist snapped with the sound of a crack from a rifle. The scarred man screamed, his body now bent double, bones sticking up and out of his broken wrist, staining the sand a deep red as blood pumped out from split and torn arteries. Alex sent his left boot at the man's head aiming for a space two feet behind it. It connected and the man's face gave way, collapsing inwards, Alex's boot pushing bone into brain into sand. As the man fell to the ground dead, Alex was already sweeping himself around to face the three remaining men. He was working on instinct now, his training taking over, no hesitation, just violence, hard and fast: the soldier was free and in control and there was nothing Alex could do about it.

Alex hurled the crook at the man to his left, the point piercing his chest and knocking him off his feet. Before the man hit the dirt, already dead, Alex was charging down the other two. They were both fumbling with their weapons, raising them to unload their magazines into their unexpected attacker, but Alex was too quick: he wrenched his crook from the chest of the man now dead on the ground and swung it hard into the face of the third man. It took off his jaw, sending it spinning off into the air as the man dropped to his knees, a gurgle of a scream bubbling out on blood spewing from his smashed face. The remaining man was tangled up with the camera strap but he managed to bring his weapon round to bear on Alex. As he went to pull the trigger, Alex closed the gap in a beat and grabbing the AK47 with his own hands, gave it a sickening twist, snapping the man's fingers then ripping them off as they stayed with the trigger guard and the rest of his hand didn't. Without a second's thought, Alex turned the weapon on its user and fired a short burst into his chest, before swinging it round on the man with no jaw. He was still screaming and Alex took off the top of his head with another short burst shutting him up for good.

As quickly as it had begun, it was over.

Alex walked over to the body of the man with the scar. His face was caved in, an unrecognisable mess of features smashed into each other by Alex's boot. Alex crouched down and rolled the body, freeing one of the man's hands and pulling from it the photo of Bonny. He held it up, brushing away dust and blood.

The sound of a laugh coughing out through blood made Alex turn to see Jackson shaking his head.

'A dog!' Jackson said, shaking his head. 'I thought he was taking the piss! But it's an actual fucking dog!'

'Patterdale Terrier,' Alex said, stuffing the photograph of Bonny into a pocket. 'Best friend I ever had.'

'No shit,' Jackson said, his head sinking back down into the sand.

Alex stood up again and looked around him. Northcutt was gone. The lieutenant and the driver were still safe in the Foxhound. And lying around him were four men dead by his hands alone, their lives ripped from them in a few short seconds of such violence that Fuller, Harper and even Jackson were now silent, despite their wounds, and staring up at Alex, the blood-spattered padre, who'd just saved their lives by killing four men. Not just because he'd had no choice, but because one of them had taken the piss out of his dog.

CHAPTER FOUR

'There's no way I can accept this, Carter, and you know it.'

Colonel James Blake was a walking recruitment ad for the army: tall, late forties, fit, the walls of his office a neat display of family photos jostling for pride of place with others of himself on numerous operations across the globe. He was standing behind a large wooden desk atop which sat a computer, a few neatly aligned pens, and some official-looking brown files. Asleep under his desk was an enormous hound the colour of chocolate that answered to the name 'Reggie'. It was part Labrador, part Rhodesian Ridgeback, had a head the size of a small car, and could, he was sure, sense an unopened can of dog food or a packet of biscuits at a distance of well over a mile. A retro style Roberts radio sat on the windowsill. In the colonel's right hand was an unopened envelope. He was leaning with his left on a shepherd's crook made of cast iron. It was a deep black in colour and speckled with flecks of rust the colour of burnt orange, which made it look as though beneath its surface a fire was raging, desperate to burst through.

'Bullshit you can't,' came the reply. Then, 'Sir.'

Alex, who was standing in front of the officer's desk, was enough years younger to make a difference, having just ghosted past his fortieth without much fanfare, a shade shorter, no less army. That much was clear if only from the stare he was giving the colonel from beneath cropped black hair shot through with grey. It was the kind of stare usually backed up by a four-man squad armed to the teeth. His uniform clearly hadn't seen an iron in a while, and instead of the expected clean-shaven face, a beard was growing wild and free; he hadn't shaved since he'd arrived back in the UK a few days ago following the ambush.

'This is the army, Carter!' the colonel said, voice raised, clearly annoyed. 'That's not how it works! As you well know.'

The colonel breathed deep, calming himself a little. 'Anyway, I can't. I'd never forgive myself. And neither would you.'

'I'm not looking for forgiveness, Sir.'

'Then what the hell are you looking for?' Blake held up the envelope. 'What's this all about, Carter? I mean, really about? Not the half-arsed excuses you'll have put in here. The truth. I know it's tough for you right now, we all do, but this isn't the answer. What happened with the patrol last month ... You had no choice. You know as well as I what would've happened if you hadn't acted as you did.'

Alex ground his teeth, his jaw hardening to stone. 'The truth, is, Sir, I'm done. That's all there is to it. I'm too much of a soldier to be a padre and too much of a padre to be a soldier. You accepting it or not makes no difference: that's my resignation.'

Alex turned to leave.

'Carter ...'

Alex reached the door. His left hand went for the handle, gave it a twist.

'Damn it, Alex!'

Hearing the colonel use his first name caused Alex to pause.

Blake spoke again, 'This isn't you, Alex. You're bigger than this. Better.'

Reggie stirred, bumped his way out from under the desk, and padded over to Alex, his nose finding his free hand. Alex was barely holding it together, tears welling up now.

'Just open it, Sir. That's all you have to do.'

Outside, the day was scratching its way into evening. Grey clouds hung in the sky torn into strips by the jet stream. Rain had been promised all day and the sky was dark.

'You could've at least come in not stinking of whatever it was you drowned yourself in last night,' Blake said. 'You're not helping yourself.'

Alex stroked the head of the massive dog that was now leaning heavily into his left leg. 'Whisky lingers, Sir,' Alex said. 'That's the point, right? Kind of numbs you to stuff.'

'And stop calling me Sir, for Christ's sake.'

'And you stop taking the Lord's name in vain.'

The colonel breathed deep and raised an eyebrow, spun the handle of the shepherd's crook in his hand, the tip sharp enough to cut a hole into the floor. 'So, you're still in there, then?' he said.

Alex laughed, but the sound had all the warmth and humour of shattered glass. 'In here?' Alex said, tapping a finger to his chest, then another to his head. 'Or here, perhaps?'

'You know what I mean.'

Alex gave the dog a last ruffle of its huge head before pulling the door open. 'To be honest, Sir –'

The colonel broke in with, 'If you call me that again, so help me God I'll ...'

Alex's face softened for the briefest of moments. 'I'm a padre, James,' he said. 'And padres don't take down four men with their own bare hands! But the worst of it all? The thing that really sticks in my throat? I enjoyed it, because they deserved it!'

Alex sucked in a breath, long and deep, then spoke again. 'I crossed a line and we both know I'd do so again in a heartbeat. It's who I am, no matter what I believe I've been called to be or to do. And that's not right. I am a risk to what this badge I now wear is supposed to represent. Which means I'm a risk to anyone I'm in theatre with. You know that as well as I.'

Colonel Blake didn't speak, knew he didn't need to.

Alex's voice was breaking on his words with the soft crash of waves upon a pebbled shore. 'I can't be a soldier and a padre,' Alex said. 'It's impossible, the weight of it ...'

'This has its own weight,' the colonel said, heaving the shepherd's crook into the air with one hand and catching it. 'You carried it easily enough. And proudly. Still can.'

Alex raised his eyes to skyward, shaking his head.

'And you saved that patrol, Alex. You! No one else. If you hadn't done what you did ...'

'I carried that to prove a point,' Alex said, nodding at the crook. 'I didn't carry it to kill, to ram it through someone's skull! That's not how this padre shit works!'

'I know,' Blake said.

'Medics, padres, we don't carry weapons with good reason: we're not supposed to be targets! I'm just lucky that things turned out the way they did.'

'Luck had nothing to do with it,' the colonel said, now balancing Alex's crook horizontally in his hand. 'Same as an SA80, right?'

'Give or take a gramme or two,' Alex said.

'What about getting another dog?' Blake said, trying again to reach into Alex and pull him back, 'I know you miss Bonny. It would do you the world of good, trust me.'

Alex didn't answer, instead just slipped out through the office door. It whispered shut behind him.

Colonel Blake slumped down into his chair and for a moment or two stared at the letter Alex had given him. Then he slipped it into the inside pocket of his jacket and with a roar of frustration, which surprised even himself, heaved the cast iron shepherd's crook like a javelin at the door. The tip slammed into the wood, the crook burying itself halfway up the shaft to hang as silent as a spear in a kill. Behind the colonel, rain peppered the windows with splashes of darkness. 'Fucking padres ...' he said.

CHAPTER FIVE

Midnight, six months later, Tora Bora Caves, Afghanistan ...

MATT HARRISON, a professional soldier since he'd left school with a reading age of seven, and a reputation for being a right cheeky bastard, looked at the three other soldiers in his fire team. Around them, sand danced into violent swirls kicked up by the blades of the helicopter, which was now chewing its way back up into the sky, having dropped them off right in the middle of a landscape you only ever went into if you were armed.

'Mission statement ...'

The three other soldiers replied in unison: 'Capture ISIL commander and bring him in for interrogation. Repeat: capture ISIL commander and bring him in for interrogation.'

The darkness around them was pure and thick despite the clear sky of stars above. Matt couldn't help but wonder if the stuff was leaking out from the cave behind them. It was a hole in a cliff just big enough to squeeze into with a stoop.

'Always feel like a total dick repeating it,' said one of the soldiers.

'We do it to make sure we all understand it and know why we're here,' Matt said. 'So stop your moaning, Wall, and wind your fucking neck in, or this job is compromised before we even begin.'

Steve Wall was small, wiry, built like a ferret, and with a face closer to a rat's than a human's, with a nose sharp enough to pierce plywood.

'Remember,' Matt said, nodding back at the cave behind them, his voice a mix of West Country and gravel, 'where we're going, these caves were used like a rabbit warren by the Taliban. Now it's ISIL. And the only way we come out of there is by following our training and being what we are. Understood?'

'Sneaky, hard bastards, right, Boss?' said another soldier who despite being called Rich Goffey, went by the nickname of Pongo thanks to the reek that haunted his feet whenever he released them from his boots. He was the largest of the other three, but didn't come close to Matt, who was touching six foot six. But it wasn't just height Matt had over them. If he wasn't on a job, down the range or on exercise, he was either at the gym or out pounding the lanes. Clothes on, he just looked tall and fit. Clothes off, he had the build of an MMA fighter.

'Professional, Goffey,' Matt said, without even a glance at the soldier.

'X-Rays?' It was Mick Fuller, the last of the soldiers, who asked this. The quietest and most unassuming of them all, he was all about the detail.

'Six,' Matt said. 'Including the target. There have been

eyes on this place for a good while before we turned up and there's been no change. Our target is a major player. Snatch and grab. That's it.'

'Quite fancy a bit of caving,' said Rich.

Steve spat on the ground. 'Join the army, they said. See the world, they said. And I end up here with you trolls exploring some fucking caves filled with ragheads. Mint.'

Rich put an arm around Steve's shoulders. 'Scared of the dark, eh, mate? Worried you'll piss yourself if a bat shits in your eye?'

'Fuck off.'

Rich stepped back. 'Just trying to be nice, and what do I get?'

'A kick in the bollocks if you keep on,' Steve said.

Matt smiled to himself. Banter was a good sign. Flushing out a cave system wasn't high on anyone's list of things to do before you die. It could get rough. Often did. It was usually humour that kept them on the right side of going insane.

'Right,' he said, reaching up for the high-power lamp on his helmet, 'we've studied where we're going, we've all got maps.' Matt tapped the plastic-covered sheet displaying spidery lines stuck to his left forearm; a detailed schematic of the system waiting for them only a few feet away. 'So let's move it and nail this bastard so we can all fuck off back to base in time for some scoff. Goffey?'

'Boss?' the soldier replied.

'You're on point.'

'Yeah, and don't get us lost,' added Steve.

As one the men followed suit with their own lamps and snapped round to face the cave entrance. Usually, for a night Op, they'd use night vision goggles (NVGs), but these still needed to pull in some light from even the most remote of sources to work. They didn't allow you to see in pure dark. So instead, it was lamps, each fitted with a red-light filter. This allowed them to see enough of what was ahead of them without sending bright beams bouncing down the tunnels to alert those they were actually there to snatch. Thermal imaging was no good either; they'd be able to see each other, but nothing of the environment around them. Not good when there was every chance of a hole appearing in the floor ready to snatch your legs from under you and drop you to your death.

Rich stepped forward, followed by Steve and Mick. Matt was tail end Charlie. Moving smoothly and quickly, the squad tabbed into the darkness, giving the impression of a giant, ferociously-armed insect slipping into its burrow.

Each soldier was armed with a C8 carbine, the shorter barrel better suited for close quarter battle in urban and other restricted environments, just like the cave they were now in. Spitting out 5.56 rounds at up to 950 rounds per minute, a thirty-round magazine didn't last long, which was why each of them carried a further 10 magazines each. A soldier could select single-shot, three-shot burst or full-auto if necessary, but the first was only of use for a rare long shot, and the third only if everything had already gone batshit crazy. Shrapnel grenades hadn't been on their shopping list for this operation, but they had plenty of flashbangs to go around. Just one would be enough to disorientate any potential enemies waiting for them. They also all carried a Glock 17, so named because it held 17 rounds, backed up with half a dozen magazines, and a combat knife each. Not that anyone wanted it to come to that. But if it did? Well, they'd been there, all of them, up close and personal. And sometimes a silent kill was necessary if a lookout could be taken out to avoid warning his pals. Strapped to their helmets were helmet cams, all with a direct feed, back to base.

With all eyes forward, Matt chinned his PRR to check comms with the team. 'Stay sharp,' he said, his voice buzzing in the others' ears. 'We don't want any surprises down here.'

'Pity,' said Rich. 'I love surprises. Can't beat a Kinder Egg, right?'

As they crept forwards, Matt thought back to some of the close quarter combat (CQC) training they'd done back home to prepare for missions just like this. The cave system, situated on some Ministry of Defence land in North Yorkshire, had been cold, muddy and wet. In fact, one exercise had taken place a little after some heavy rain and they'd spent most of it up to their waists in icy water. Some parts of that cave had been little more than belly crawls in the mud and, as their commanding officer (CO) had pointed out, they'd come out at the end of it looking like they'd been shat out of a dinosaur's arse. Their kit had ended up wrecked, weapons jammed, and the training officer had found the whole thing pissing hilarious. The caves out in Afghanistan, though, were nothing like those back home, which were either wet, muddy, or both. Instead, they were dry as bone, in places the rock crumbling as they brushed past. It was the bugs though, which Matt hated. Scorpions and camel spiders called these places home and it was the spiders he hated more than anything. A fire fight with grenades and mortars landing all around he was fine with compared to coming face-to-face with one of those ugly, big-fanged fuckers. And they weren't actually even spiders, just some massive mutant bug dreamt up by evolution to give you eternal nightmares even when you were awake.

Matt pulled himself back into the moment and focused

on what he could see in the eerie red light spilling out from the lamp clamped onto his helmet. The tunnel itself was narrow, at points forcing them to turn sideways and crab-walk their way through. Although they were going ever downwards, the roof wasn't following in the same way, and the fissure rose higher and higher above their heads. The air was dry, tinged with the sweaty tang of animals that had used the place for shelter, no doubt for centuries, perhaps even thousands of years, Matt thought.

Rich popped a clenched fist up by the side of his head, stopped dead. His voice cracked through on the PRR. 'Something ahead, Boss.'

The four men stood statue-still, not even their breath making a sound.

A voice, faint but odd and out of place in the cathedral-like quiet of the cave, tumbled over them from somewhere ahead of where they were stood.

Matt turned his attention to the map on his arm, quickly identifying where they were. If he was correct, then the voice was coming from a chamber which opened out about fifty metres ahead of where they were now standing.

Matt told the others and they all checked their own maps to confirm.

The voices came again. They sounded agitated, which wasn't a good sign. Matt recognised the odd word. Whoever it was, they were speaking Pashtu. Matt knew that everything was about to go from zero to a hundred in a beat.

Matt signalled for the squad to edge forward. They maintained close formation, covering each other, ready to burst out into whatever faced them and bring it to the enemy without warning or quarter. Bringing back someone alive wasn't exactly the same as bringing someone back uninjured and Matt's focus wasn't just on the mission statement, but on getting them all back alive having fulfilled it.

As they drew closer, Matt noticed other sounds join the voices; heavy objects being dragged. The red light from their torches slid along the rocks around and ahead of them like flames licking up a wall.

Rich stopped again. 'They're round the next bend, Boss,' he said, his voice barely a whisper on the PRR.

Steve said, 'And here's me not even in my DJ.'

No one laughed.

'Goffey: flashbang!' Matt ordered.

Rich pulled an unassuming canister from his webbing kit, and was about to pull the pin, when the voices ahead of them turned to screams.

CHAPTER SIX

0600HRS, TORA BORA CAVES, AFGHANISTAN …

CORPORAL RACHEL COATES, an Army medic who'd been in too many years to remember what life was like before her wardrobe was all camo and combat boots, was racing into hell, running full pelt away from a Chinook helicopter kitted-out to do field surgery on the move. She was stooped against the downdraft from the twin rotors, powering herself forwards on sprinter's legs, the wind doing all it could to snatch at the few strands of her hair she'd not managed to stuff under her helmet. A few years ago those legs had helped her run away from the gangs that had ripped the heart out of her community back home in London. If she'd stayed, she'd have joined. Instead, she'd run, and kept running, and her legs were strong now, iron.

Blasting out from under the downdraft, Rachel kept running, shielding her eyes from the dust. Wherever she was, she didn't care: it was just another rock-strewn part of the same rock-strewn landscape she'd almost got used to since starting yet another tour a couple of months ago. All that mattered was what she would find at the end of her sprint.

Rachel mentally checked off all the kit she was carrying with her and what she'd do to assess the situation when she arrived. That didn't mean simply any injuries to deal with. She had to think about potential threats to herself, her team and the soldiers they'd been sent in to Medevac out; IEDs, enemy combatants, hell, even the fucking wildlife wanted to kill you.

Less than an hour ago she'd been yanked out of a sexy dream involving her new boyfriend, a bottle of Prosecco, and some red silk straps which had had her restrained on a bed. It wasn't something they'd ever done, but she rather liked the idea now, thanks to the way little more than a dream had made her feel. Within minutes of being woken, she and the rest of the medical team had been in the air, the report of what they were heading off to deal with broken and garbled. Something about a small team being compromised. Small teams always – always – meant the same thing: Special Forces lads sent off to do sneaky-beaky stuff that no one ever heard about. Unless, of course, everything went either epically shit or epically heroic, and the tabloids caught wind of it. Throw in something particularly gruesome and the public would go crazy, such as that SAS trooper she'd read about who'd taken to the enemy with a spade and decapitated one of them. The mad bastard. Or the squad of French paratroopers skinned alive by the Taliban ...

Rachel saw cliffs ahead. Her legs were burning now but she kept on pumping hard. She'd lost soldiers before. It was a part of the job she knew she would never get used to. She didn't want to either: she ran because someone else's life depended on it. That's why she trained hard, not just for distance, but speed; it had fuck all to do with getting a six pack.

The cliffs were close now. Rachel saw a black hole squatting moodily at the base of them: a cave entrance. She shuddered. She knew there were people who explored caves for fun. That was one thing. Heading into them against an armed enemy, though? That was something else. She had no idea how anyone did it. Reminded her of things she'd read about soldiers in Vietnam heading into the tunnels with little more than a torch, knife and pistol. Insanity.

The path ahead dipped, taking the cave just out of sight. Rachel sped down a slope, her legs in a blur beneath her, up the other side, broke the horizon.

A soldier was standing at the cave entrance. Every bit of him was covered in blood like he'd been painted with the stuff. White eyes, wide with burning terror, stared out from a face almost black with gore. His fatigues were dripping wet, blood pooling at his feet. He wasn't screaming so much as roaring, the sound of it tearing around the cliffs above, trying to escape. In his arms Rachel could see the body of another soldier, or what was left of one. It looked like a rag doll puppet chucked from a moving car, all broken and limp and smashed.

As Rachel skidded to a halt in front of the soldier two other medics came alongside.

'What in the name of mother fuck ...?'

Rachel wasn't in the mood for a discussion, and after ordering the two medics to pull themselves together and have a look-see to check if there were any others – there had been four in the team after all, so where were the other two? – was eyes on the soldier in front of her.

'We're here to help,' she said, dropping her kit bag to the ground, voice calm, eyes on the soldier's own. 'Lay your friend down and let us do our job. Where are the others? We were told there were four of you.'

The soldier wasn't listening, just raging, staring like a wild bull.

'Listen to me!' Rachel upped her volume, trying to get his attention. 'We're here to –'

The soldier flung the body he was holding at the two medics. It slapped into them both with enough force to send them sprawling, blood spraying into the air. Bits tore off, spinning into the dust. Then he was round and into Rachel.

Rachel was hardwired to the moment. She saw a right hook racing at her, dodged it easily, stepped back, open hands up in defence, but just as ready to bring it if the need arose.

'Calm the fuck down!' she yelled, as the soldier stumbled, trying to steady himself after the wild swing of his fist. 'We're medics! We need to treat you and get you back home, okay? And you need to tell us what happened: where is the rest of your team?'

The soldier snarled. The sound wasn't human. It had an echo to it, Rachel noticed, a resonance that seemed to rumble from all around them, like the very ground and cliffs were joining in.

From the corner of her eye, Rachel saw the other two medics struggling with what was now clearly a corpse, the body broken, smashed, ripped and torn, by what she hadn't the faintest idea. Wounds like that were usually found on bits of bodies after an IED or a mortar, something explosive. For a body to remain intact and to still take that kind of damage; what would do that? And how?

Movement to her right snatched Rachel back into the

moment and she turned to see the soldier charging her. Whatever his injuries were she didn't know and right now didn't care. She needed to get him under control to have any chance at sorting this situation out and getting them the hell out of there. For all she knew whoever had done this to them was closing in so they needed to exit fast.

With a quick shuffle back, Rachel was out of the way as the soldier closed in. Watching him stumble past, she went with him, forced his momentum to take him to the ground, and was on him immediately, pinning him to the dirt. He may have had a weight advantage, but she had him in a hold that with any movement would snap his arm.

'Stop!' Rachel screamed, straining against the struggling soldier beneath her. 'I'm a medic! Calm the fuck down!'

At last, the soldier relaxed.

'That's better,' Rachel said. 'Now –'

The soldier rolled out from beneath her, was on top of her now, his hands at her throat, crushing it.

Rachel choked back shock with a gargled cry. The soldier stared at her through eyes bloodshot and filled with fury. Rachel tried to hook the hands away, but his grip was like a bear trap. And he was mumbling at her, words tumbling from his mouth that made no sense. It wasn't English, wasn't Pashtu. Whatever it was, Rachel hadn't a clue, but it kept on coming, a tirade of snarls and sentences that ripped at the air around them, his teeth biting and snapping at them as they spilled out of his throat. She could sense that she was losing consciousness, sparks bursting on the edge of her vision. Desperately she grabbed at him, tried to hook onto anything that would give her an advantage, some way to flip the mad bastard off. Then she noticed that in the struggle some of the blood covering the soldier had been smeared away and there, staring at her, was the soldier's name and number.

Rachel hacked in a last desperate breath and screamed the name: 'HARRISON!'

The soldier froze and the words stopped. Rachel saw his face twitch as he shook his head like he was trying to dislodge something from inside his skull. Then he squeezed his eyes shut and, letting Rachel go for a moment, balled his fists into them before dropping his hands to his sides. When he snapped his eyes back open, Rachel saw something staring at her from behind them: a thing of flame and darkness and rage so violent her skin crawled under its glare.

Rachel dug deep, somehow found some energy, and pushed it all downwards to thrust up with her left knee. The impact sent the soldier into the air. Crushed groin or not, she didn't care: she could breathe again and, to make sure he didn't come back at her, Rachel sent her left elbow in a hard sweep across his face. She didn't aim at it, instead she aimed through it: this fucker was going down, those bastard demon eyes and all. The elbow connected, and the soldier dropped to her side like a plank.

Rachel sat up and, gasping for breath, grabbed her medical bag to shuffle over to the soldier, her fists up ready for another attack.

None came.

It was over.

Whatever hellish light she'd seen in those eyes had been snuffed out. Just another day at the office, Rachel thought, breath burning her bruised throat. Then, locking away what had just happened into that place where she kept all the horrors she had witnessed as an army medic, with blood-covered hands, she went to work.

CHAPTER SEVEN

Colonel James Blake forced his eyes open like a man woken from a coma and stared at his office. His head throbbed. The clock on his desk told him it was later than even the dark outside his window suggested. Where had the last two hours gone, he thought? He'd been catching up on admin, the not-so-sexy stuff that all the promotional material about life in the military forgets to mention. There had been a few meetings to tick even fewer boxes, a dodgy lunch. And he'd been looking forward to finishing up and heading home to a steak and a decent bottle of wine, not least because it was a lovely, bright spring day and he rather fancied seeing it out with a cigar in his garden. Then what? Rubbing his eyes, he pulled open a desk drawer and grabbed a bottle of whisky knowing that a good slug of the stuff wouldn't necessarily jog his memory, but it would at least make him feel better. Grabbing a glass, he poured a two-finger slug of Laphroaig. He'd bought himself a bottle of the 1815 a year ago and had been saving it for a special occasion. Cost over a hundred quid, too, and he was still smarting from that. This wasn't exactly a special occasion, but the upside of that was that this whisky made every occasion special. And that's what he told himself as he took a sip, only to have the sweet, smoky burn of the whisky turned sour by an explosion of pain in his mind. He dropped the glass, winced, squeezed his eyes shut, but the pain kept on coming, driving into him like nails, and for a moment it seemed to him that his office was aflame, that he could smell the sweet rich stench of heat and burning so close he was sure he would soon be on fire himself. Then the pain stopped, he glanced up at his laptop, and saw the email.

The message itself, all in capital letters, was the very definition of brief: 'SEE ATTACHED'. He checked the sender's email address and didn't recognise it. However, if it had got through the security which, by necessity, cloaked anything to do with computers in his line of work, then it had to be legit. So, with his head still groggy from the unplanned nap at his desk, his mouth burning from the whisky, and his brain still unable to digest either the pain or the strange sensation of burning, Colonel James Blake clicked open the attachment before he'd even had a chance to even think what he was doing. But by that point it didn't really matter.

The attachment was a folder containing zipped files and documents, each with a name: Harrison; Wall; Goffey; Fuller; Coates. The first four were video files and he watched the first in shocked silence, knowing at the end of it that there was nowhere in his head he could ever safely store away what he'd seen and forget about it. With shaking fingers, he then clicked open the other three files, each of them piling on the horror in spades. Finally, he clicked through the documents, each one giving a detailed biography of the soldiers involved, one of whom – Harrison – the colonel was surprised to read, had served with his padre,

Alex Carter, in the years before the soldier had turned to God. Since their last conversation, the colonel had given Carter extended leave in the hope that some time out would give him a chance to come to his senses. And since then he'd kept an eye on him. That was his job, after all; to make sure the people under his command were okay, even when they weren't officially on duty. The padre had certainly been keeping himself busy, Blake thought, but wasn't so sure what he was doing with his time was helping his head in any way at all. But each to their own, right? And arguing with a padre was never easy.

Blake was a man of combat. He'd seen action in Bosnia, Iraq and Afghanistan. He knew what it was like to be shot at, blown up, even stabbed. He'd seen exactly what war, big and small, could do to the fragile human body and the even more fragile human mind. War was a wall and if you threw a body at it hard enough no amount of Kevlar would prevent the inevitable: it would break. More often than not, it would shatter and split and burst into a million different pieces, none of which would ever go back together again in the right order. It was a violent, scarlet-coloured hell and he knew that he was damned lucky to have survived it at all. Others hadn't. Close friends lost to the violence of war in theatre, or chased by its horrors all the way back home to suicide once it was over. But all the shitholes he'd been up to his neck in blood and bullets in didn't help him to make any sense of what was now playing out on his laptop screen.

Another whisky was calling him but he ignored it. Instead, Blake clicked on the final file, 'Coates'. The document, a witness testimony from a corporal, provided a written account of the aftermath of what Blake had seen on the videos, but was no less harrowing or baffling because of it. Reading only seemed to make it worse, his mind conjuring up images described by Coates in graphic technicolour.

Leaning back in his chair and closing his eyes, Blake reached down with his left hand as Reggie, blissfully unaware of the worries that buzzed around in his owner's head, nuzzled in. The colonel didn't know what to think. On the one hand, he was still reeling from the shock of what he'd seen and read. On the other, he was more than a little put out that someone had sent him the document anonymously. His email address wasn't exactly public knowledge.

Blake leant forward and typed, 'Who is this, how did you get my email address, and what does any of this have to do with me?'

A reply pinged its arrival barely seconds later: 'You will know soon enough.'

The colonel was shocked and angry.

'I have forwarded your email to those with greater skills than I at finding out,' he typed, his fingers hammering at the keyboard. 'This is clearly classified information and you should not be party to it.'

'No, you haven't,' came the reply, then, 'Call Coates. Send Carter.'

And that was it. And on reading them the colonel was none the wiser and all the more confused. He laughed, but the sound was cold and unamused. He didn't like having his leg pulled at the best of times, but this was worse because it was sick. The videos, the witness testimony, all showed that something terrible had happened and soldiers had died. Whoever this prankster was, and where they'd stolen the data from, he had no idea, but he was absolutely sure he wanted them gone.

'I am now forwarding this email, and its contents, to people you've never heard of but whom you will, I'm sure, soon be very well acquainted with,' the colonel typed. 'Good evening.'

He was tempted to just type, 'Fuck off', but that didn't strike him as entirely professional, though it did accurately express exactly how he felt.

When the reply came, it contained only a link to a location on Google Maps. Underneath it were the same instructions about Coates and Carter.

The location meant nothing to Blake and the phone number he didn't recognise. It was the mentioning again of Coates and Carter that made him pause. That the person on the other end of these messages knew who he was, knew about Coates, well that was concerning, but Carter? That simply made no sense. The man had been out of action for six months and the events from the fateful patrol were shut down and locked away for good. His only link was to one of the soldiers, but that was from years ago. And what soldier in the army couldn't link themselves to goodness knows how many others courtesy of the numerous moves from base to base, operation to operation? That was just a part of normal soldiering life!

The colonel glanced back at his laptop screen to see that a new message had appeared. He clicked it open.

It said, 'Remember Kosovo.'

The words slammed into Blake like a wrecking ball to the sound in his head of a young girl, her face pulled taught by a laugh that became a scream that eventually tore her face to shreds and it was all he could do to not fall off his chair.

No one knew about Kosovo. No one! Not even his wife! What the hell was this? Who the hell ...

The colonel's earlier thoughts about reporting the emails, the contents, stalled. And all because of that one word, Kosovo. It had sent his blood cold and opened a door to nightmares he had thought were long ago left behind. Clearly they weren't, but not only that, the secret of what that word meant to him at least, was obviously not a secret. And that didn't just have him nervous, it had him terrified, so terrified that he was sure right then he could smell and taste the memory of what had happened all those years ago.

He had no choice, it seemed. Reporting this to the appropriate people would mean all of that being once again dragged up. He couldn't afford for that to happen, not because it would ruin his career so much as destroy his sanity, something which he'd only barely managed to stitch together into some sense of passable normality in the days after.

There was only one person the colonel would be calling now and he didn't give a shit how pissed off that person would be.

He picked up his desk phone and punched in the number.

CHAPTER EIGHT

'WHO IS THIS?'

The voice was firm, Blake thought. Assured. If what he'd just read was the witness testimony of someone sane, then it only added to the validity of what he'd been sent. And that was deeply unnerving.

'This is Colonel Blake. I'm based in –'

'What's this about? I've a training session this evening and I'm heading out in five.'

Blake sucked in a deep breath. Not because he was irritated at Coates' abruptness, but to gather himself before he spoke. Once the words were out, this was real, what he'd seen and read, was real, and he was taking it seriously. But then the mention of Kosovo had confirmed all of that, hadn't it? Christ alive, what was he getting pulled into ...

'Then I'll be quick.' The colonel quickly briefed Rachel on the email he'd received, the files, what he'd seen, what he'd read.

'I've nothing more to add,' Rachel said. 'And to be honest I'd rather just forget all about it. Now, if you don't mind, I need to get going.'

'But I do,' Blake said. 'I mind a great deal.' He was about to tell the medic to cancel her training and to come and see him in his office immediately, when he had another idea.

'I will be with you in thirty minutes,' he said.

'Impossible,' Rachel replied. 'I've training to do, like I said. Can't this wait till tomorrow?'

'No,' Blake replied. 'Thirty minutes. Be ready.'

Blake hung up before Rachel had a chance to reply. He was at Rachel's door 26 minutes later.

Rachel stood in the doorway of her small army-built house facing the colonel with a stare he had a feeling could melt steel. 'What's this about?'

'I'll explain on the way,' Blake said, turning from the door, making it clear that Rachel had no choice but to follow. He jabbed a finger at his vehicle. 'Get in.'

Swinging himself into the driving seat of his Range Rover, he had the engine purring as Rachel climbed in next to him and clipped herself in.

'You got a Barbour jacket on the back seat as well?' Rachel asked, mouth barely hiding a sneer.

'Yeah, and a chocolate brown lab-cross: he's in the back guarding the shotguns.'

'Figures,' Rachel said as a growl from the rear of the vehicle made her turn her head to see Reggie, his massive head peering over the rear seat from the boot of the Range Rover, doing his best to look aggressive. Instead he just looked like he was passing wind.

Blake heaved the vehicle away from the roadside and punched it. The Range Rover, despite its ungainly size, took off at speed.

'So, Colonel,' Rachel said, 'are you going to tell me where you're taking me, or is this a mystery tour for one?'

'You always like this?'

Rachel's dead-eye stare response said it all and Blake let silence hang between them for a while.

'Corporal,' Blake said at last, and now half an hour into what he reckoned would be a ninety-minute journey, 'about your witness testimony ...'

'Look,' Rachel said, 'I've told you: I've nothing to add to it. The incident was only a few days before my tour ended and now I'm back here with more than enough to be getting on with. So why don't you just tell what it has to do with you abducting me in the middle of the night?'

'I didn't abduct you,' Blake said. 'You came of your own accord. And it's not the middle of the night, it's still early evening.'

'You're a colonel, so I couldn't exactly say no,' Rachel said. 'And it will be the middle of the night by the time we get back from wherever the hell it is we're going.'

Blake did his best to hide a smile. Coates, he was quickly realising, was someone very much in charge of her own destiny. He liked that in a person. He liked it a lot.

'We're going to visit someone,' Blake said. 'Someone I think should look at what I was sent this evening.'

'And I have to be here why?'

'Like you said,' Blake said with a smile, 'I'm a colonel.'

Rachel simply shook her head in response and turned to stare out of the window.

The rest of the journey passed by with no further words spoken, the hypnotising hum of the tyres on the road the only sound.

When they arrived at their destination, Rachel, if it could be at all possible, seemed even more unimpressed. 'Where the fuck are we?' Then, remembering in who's company she was, she added a less than enthusiastic, 'Sir ...'

Blake stared out into darkness. The beams of his headlights showed a bleak landscape of moorland beyond a gate held together by bailer twine and hope. In the middle distance was a stone barn and, parked around it, a dozen or so vehicles.

'We're at an illegal bare-knuckle fight,' the colonel said. 'And the person we need to talk to is in that barn kicking the living shit out of someone. Coming?'

Rachel raised an eyebrow. 'That the best you can do for a cover story?'

Blake shrugged and got out of the vehicle. He didn't wait: he knew Rachel was following.

Approaching the barn, Blake heard voices carried to them on the wind, which was clearly gearing up to turn into a full-on gale in the next few hours. He could smell rain on it, too, and he really didn't want to be out here when it hit.

Drawing closer, the voices grew clearer, turning into shouts and cheers. At the door to the barn, Blake stopped and turned to Rachel. 'You ready?'

Rachel's eyes flicked from the colonel to the barn and back to the colonel. 'For what?'

'Let me do the talking,' Blake said. 'We just need to get him alone and I don't want him bolting like a rabbit.'

At that, Blake pushed through a door in the side of the barn and led Rachel into a flickering darkness on the other side.

Inside, the darkness and shadows of the barn danced with a soft light slipping from a random collection of battery-powered lanterns hung around the walls. Remnants of the barn's previous activity and occupants were scattered across the floor: small piles of straw and tufts of wool brushed aside for what was happening in the centre of the building.

A small crowd was gathered, all of them wrapped up

against the cold in large jackets. A mostly male crowd, though the colonel could see a number of women scattered about. The air was a mix of breath condensing in the chill of the night and cigarette and cigar smoke. No one was vaping, he noticed, perhaps because it was impossible to watch what was going on at the centre of the crowd and carry off a plastic stick jutting out of your mouth with sufficient meanness.

'What the hell is this, Colonel?' Rachel hissed into his ear, but Blake held up his hand to shush her then motioned for her to follow him.

Squeezing through the crowd, Blake hid himself behind a hardened scowl, one he'd perfected over the years and used to great effect. Then, just a couple of steps from the activity drawing everyone's attention, someone stepped in front of him.

'The fuck are you?' The man in Blake's way was all menace, eyes narrowed in a face of weathered skin like rips in leather. He was wearing a flat cap, his hands shoved deep into the pockets of a tatty waxed jacket which stretched painfully across a large stomach.

He looked, Blake thought, like the kind of person who, when not watching an illegal bare knuckle fight, enjoyed dog fighting and badger baiting. He'd never met the man in person until now, but he'd done a little digging over the past six months. Force of habit as much as anything; he knew the importance of intel.

Blake raised his left hand in front of the man's face so that he could see the roll of notes clasped in it. 'Mr Rudd,' he said, enjoying the confused look on the man's face at hearing his name from the mouth of a stranger. 'Here's two hundred.'

Rudd raised an eyebrow, the sight of the money quickly turning the look of confusion to one of greed. 'Which fighter, Mr ...?' he asked, fishing for a name.

Blake glanced briefly over the man's left shoulder to see two men facing off. Both were bare-chested. One was built like a bull and had hair the colour of rust, the other was wiry and lean and his head was shaved to stubble.

'The one who's head looks like a bollock,' Blake said, purposefully neglecting to give his name to Rudd. 'My money says he knocks out the other fighter and that I have to drag him out of here before he kills someone.' Blake looked Rudd up and down then added, 'Probably you.'

Rudd's grin split into a laugh. 'You like to throw money away, I'm happy to oblige,' he said, taking the notes from the colonel's hands. 'That skinny runt must have a death wish to go up against Basher.'

'He choose that name or you?' Blake asked, barely able to hide a smirk.

'Had it since school,' Rudd said, then leant in close enough for Blake to smell the man's teeth and added, 'on account of him being a hard cunt.'

Blake said nothing in reply and instead edged past the man and towards the fighters. He could sense the corporal close behind him, but at that moment he was focused on what was playing out in the middle of the crowd.

The two men were in the centre of a circle drawn out in chalk on the flagstone floor. Blake guessed at it being six metres in diameter, so just enough space for them to lay into each other without bringing the crowd into the action as well.

Judging by the fact that neither of them were as yet out of breath, the fight had only just started. That and the fact that both men were circling each other, trying to get a measure of his opponent.

Basher, Blake could tell, was already confident. He was smiling, a gum shield decorated with the word 'NAILS' on it showing between his lips. He was a big bastard, of that there was no doubt, towering over his opponent, and in an arm wrestle he'd have the upper hand easily. He carried a physique built on weights and throwing straw bales and sacks of animal feed around, but fed on a diet of fry ups. There was muscle, and a lot of it, and there was fat, the man's belly a pallid white monstrosity. The crowd had clearly already decided who their money was on and Basher was enjoying himself, trying to goad the other fighter into making a mistake before the scrap had even had chance to warm up.

The other fighter was the absolute opposite. Wiry and lean he seemed utterly oblivious to those gathered in the barn to watch two men kick the living shit out of each other. He was relaxed, his guard up to show not two fists but instead open palms. And whereas Basher's torso was a giant version of the Pillsbury Doughboy, his was that of someone who could probably run for hours carrying a man on his back, a back which betrayed scars, that on closer inspection Blake knew would tell tales of bullet, knife and shrapnel wounds. There were other scars, too, Blake noticed. They were faint, but visible; a row of oddly circular marks which stretched down across the man's torso.

'This is illegal.' It was Rachel's voice in Blake's ear.

'A good many things are,' he replied. 'But it's not as though it stops them from happening.'

'What the hell does this have to do with my witness testimony?' Rachel said, then yanked the colonel around to face her. 'Colonel or not, you'd better tell me now or –'

Basher roared, drowning out whatever it was Rachel was saying and Blake snapped his eyes back around to the fight to see the huge mass of the man lunge for the other fighter. A beat before Basher was on him, his opponent side stepped and at the same time swung an open palm across Basher's exposed right ear. The sound of the slap cut the noise of the crowd to silence as Basher stumbled then howled.

'Holy shit ...' Rachel said.

'Quite,' Blake replied, smiling to himself about just how strangely true her words were.

Basher was now standing in the centre of the ring, his right hand clasped over his ear, screaming obscenities, phlegm catapulting from his mouth and onto the floor. He charged again, this time with his fists up ready to knock his opponent's head clean off his shoulders. At least that's what Blake thought the man believed he was about to do, only to find that his punches were dodged and deflected with ease.

The crowd, woken now from their initial shock at seeing Basher get slapped, erupted and the air was smashed apart with cries and yells of people baying for blood.

Basher kept on with his attack, swinging his arms wildly, swearing and spitting all the more, sweat beading across his body.

'Come here you little shit! I'm going to kill you, you hear? You're fucking dead!'

Basher's verbal attacks garnered approval from the crowd and a couple of the spectators stepped over the chalked line on the floor and pushed the smaller fighter towards him. Basher grabbed him with both arms and lifted the man off his feet only to have his nose smashed in by his opponent's skull. It exploded, sending blood into the air and over anyone unfortunate enough to be too close to the action.

Basher, rage taking over, dropped the man to the ground and hurled a kick directly at his stomach only to have his ankle connect with a raised boot.

Judging by the agony that tore across his face, Blake guessed that whatever rules in place for this fight were about to be torn to pieces.

Basher, limping now, barged his way through the crowd to a holdall shoved up against the wall. Before anyone realised what was happening, he had yanked out a cricket bat. Spitting his mouth guard to the floor, he wiped the blood from his face and made his way back into the circle.

'I'm going to crack your skull like a fuckin' coconut, you little runt!'

Basher raised the cricket bat behind his head. Calls of, 'Kill him, Bash!' and 'Brain the little bastard!' chimed from the crowd.

'You have to stop this!' Rachel said. 'We have to do something! He'll kill him!'

'Most probably,' Blake said.

Basher swung the bat and it whistled through the air barely an inch from his opponent's face. Then, when he heaved it back to have another go, the other fighter stepped in fast and close, his left arm up and blocking the swing, his right jabbing in and under Basher's jaw.

What happened next was too fast for anyone to follow, but the cricket bat was broken out of Basher's hand and another slap, this time to his left ear, dropped the massive man to his knees.

Choking, blood streaming from his nose and down his chest, his wrist hanging helpless, no doubt broken, Blake suspected, Basher tried to pull himself to his feet only to find himself in a choke hold, his opponent now behind him, his right arm bent under his chin, his left gripping it hard to add to the pressure. Basher's legs kicked, his eyes bulged, then his whole body went slack. The other fighter eased off the pressure, stood up, and Basher slumped to the ground unconscious. Then he let out a snore, followed by a fart, and pissed himself.

CHAPTER NINE

For a moment, the crowd was silent, eyes all staring at the mess of Basher on the dirty flagstone floor.

The winning fighter moved away from Basher to push through the crowd, but no one moved.

'He's just unconscious,' the fighter said. 'He'll wake up in a minute or two and have a killer headache, but he'll be fine.'

'What about his wrist?' someone said, a finger jabbing at the fighter. 'You broke it! You broke his fucking wrist!'

Another said, 'We came here to see a scrap, mate, and you cut it too short.'

Shouts of agreement cascaded into the moment and Blake was sensing that the crowd was turning just a little bit hostile.

The fighter turned away from those in front of him and made to walk across the circle to push through at the other side only to be met by the man who had welcomed the colonel and Rachel to the proceedings. Rudd was chewing a cigar and holding Basher's cricket bat. He raised it so that the end of it rested against the fighter's chest. He then gave it a little jab knocking the fighter back just enough to get his attention. 'Where you going, son?'

'Home,' the fighter replied.

'And you think you can just walk out of here, do you?' Rudd laughed and glanced around the crowd.

'Once I've got my winnings, yes. I won. That's how this works.'

Rudd's laugh died. 'I'd heard you were a cocky little shit,' he said, and jabbed again with the bat. 'That's why I set this fight up, right? Teach you a lesson. Fucking outsiders coming in, thinking they can mix it up with folk like us! That's not how this works, mate, you hear me?'

The fighter nodded back at Basher who was now beginning to stir. 'Didn't work out too well for you then, did it?'

'Who said the lesson was over?' Rudd said. 'Pity about Basher, really, but I guess sometimes you've just got to do these things yourself, right?'

Rudd jabbed again with the cricket bat, only this time the fighter twisted and the bat slid across his chest. Rudd stumbled forwards. As he did so, the fighter snatched the cricket bat out of Rudd's hand and, with a quick shove, helped Rudd on his way past him. Finally, with a sharp kick of his left foot at Rudd's feet, the fighter sent him crashing down onto the flagstones next to Basher.

'My money,' the fighter said, resting the cricket bat on Rudd's heaving gut. 'Now.'

The crowd were silent again, glaring death at the fighter.

'You want your money?' Rudd said, climbing back to his feet and picking his cigar off the floor to shove back into his mouth.

To Blake's surprise, Rudd, now on his feet, turned to

square off against the fighter. 'What say I just keep it and you fuck right off?'

A click sounded and everyone's eyes were drawn to what Rudd had in his hands pointed at the fighter's chest: a double-barrelled 12 gauge, sawn off about eight inches in front of the trigger guard. One of the hammers was pulled back and Rudd's fingers were resting on the two triggers.

The fighter didn't move, just stared.

'Thought so,' Rudd said, a smile creasing his mouth, his confidence given a shot of adrenaline by the presence of the weapon in his hand. 'So here's an idea: before you leave, what say we let Basher have another swing or two at you? How'd you like that?'

Rudd gave a short nod to two men behind the fighter and they moved to grab him. Before they had a chance, the fighter was already moving towards Rudd and they were left grasping at an empty space. With a speed only the colonel, of all the people in that space, had seen before, the fighter brought his left hand round into the shotgun, sweeping it away from pointing at him at the same time as jamming the cocked hammer with the fleshy part of his hand between his wrist and little finger. Pushing the shotgun in hard against Rudd, forcing him to stumble backwards, he sent a flurry of punches into the man's face, busting his nose as he had done Basher's, before bringing the hand down to grab the shotgun's barrel. With a sickening twist, he broke it out of the man's hands with such violence that it tore away Rudd's trigger finger and sent it skidding across the floor. With blood pumping from the wound and from his smashed face, Rudd stumbled backwards and into Basher, dropping onto him like a sack of potatoes to crack Basher's head against the flagstones with a dull thud.

The fighter stood over both men, the shotgun levelled at their faces. His face was calm, but his eyes smouldered with a dark heat.

Rudd held up his hands. 'Don't! Don't fucking shoot! You can have your money! Just take it! Take it and fuck off!'

The fighter made no move towards the men, just eased back first one hammer on the shotgun, then the other.

'Please don't kill me!' Rudd yelled, his voice breaking on his words with panic. 'Please!'

Basher was still too dazed to realise exactly what was going on and was just staring at the shotgun as though trying to work out what it was.

Rudd was about to speak again when a voice cried out, 'Enough!'

It was Blake, but the fighter didn't turn to face him. Instead, he eased back the hammers, broke the shotgun and tipped it over to drop the cartridges from the barrels onto the floor, before stripping the weapon in front of Rudd and Basher's eyes and scattering the parts across the floor. He then reached down and with a quick search of Rudd's jacket pulled out a wad of cash from which he pulled a sizeable number of notes before handing the rest to someone in the crowd. Then, without a word, he pushed through the crowd, which opened for him without resistance, and made his way to a rucksack near the door. He was pulling on a shirt when Blake stepped up behind him.

'What are you doing here, Sir?' the fighter asked.

'I've been asking that exact same question since we arrived,' Rachel said, standing between Blake and the fighter, arms folded across her chest.

'Corporal Coates,' Blake said, 'allow me to introduce to you my favourite army padre, Alex Carter.'

CHAPTER TEN

Corporal Coates stared at the man in front of her. 'You're a padre?'

'Was,' Alex said, fully clothed now, the rucksack heaved onto his back.

'Still are, actually,' said the colonel.

Rachel eyed up the man in front of her. 'But you were just ... I mean, that was a bare knuckle fight, right? And you were ...' Rachel's voice faded and she looked back at Rudd and Basher who were still on the floor.

The rest of the crowd was dispersing now, slipping back out into the black storm which sounded as though it was doing its best to tear the barn out of its old foundations.

'We need to talk,' Blake said as Alex made to leave. 'There's something I need you to have a look at.'

'No, there isn't,' Alex said. 'And next time you decide you want to spy on me, have the courtesy to ask first.'

'Then that wouldn't exactly be spying, would it?' Blake said.

'Exactly,' Alex said and walked out through the door.

Rachel glanced over at the colonel. 'He's a padre?' she

said. 'He just nearly killed two men and he's a fucking padre? How is that even a thing?'

Blake shrugged. 'Takes all sorts to make a world, Corporal,' he said. 'And you don't need to worry; he wouldn't have killed them.'

'How can you be so sure?'

'Because they were never a threat,' Blake said, and pushed through the door.

Outside, and buffeted by rain coming at him like a swarm of angry wasps, the colonel caught up with Alex, who was about to climb into his car.

'I need your help, Alex,' Blake said, reaching out to ease the car door shut again. 'Something's come up. I don't ... I can't ... Look, can we talk? I think you'd –'

'Whatever it is,' Alex said, cutting the colonel off, 'I'm the last person you need helping you.'

'Exactly,' Blake said. 'You are the last person because there isn't anyone else. Not with your skill set, your background.'

Rachel joined them. 'So you didn't think to let him know we were coming? Brilliant planning, Colonel. Thanks for the wasted night.'

Alex tried to open his car door but the colonel kept enough pressure on it to make sure that he couldn't. Not yet.

'Remember what you said in my office a few months ago? About you being too much of a soldier to be a padre and too much of a padre to be a soldier?'

Alex said nothing, just stared at the colonel.

'Well right now I need both parts, Alex. I need the padre and the soldier. They're both who and what you are. Please ...'

With that, Colonel Blake eased off on the car door and

Alex opened it and climbed in, clipping himself in and sparking the engine into life.

'There are better ways to deal with what you've been through than this,' Blake said, leaning in for a final word and dropping onto Alex's lap a folded sheet of A4 paper he'd pulled from a pocket. 'Just read this, please? I'll wait for your call.'

'Then you'll be waiting a long time,' Alex said and with that he slammed the car door, slipped the vehicle into gear, and headed off back down the lane.

'What was that you gave him?' Rachel asked as they both stared after the disappearing rear lights of Alex's car.

'Your witness testimony,' Blake said.

'And you think he'll read it?'

'Yes,' the colonel replied, 'and when he does he'll be in my office quicker than that ginger gorilla hit dirt back there in the barn.'

'What makes you so sure?'

Colonel Blake let out a long, deep sigh. 'He served with the survivor of the team you brought back from that cave.'

'Can't have done,' Rachel said. 'He's a padre.'

'That he is,' the colonel said. 'But before he wore the cross, corporal, he wore something else.'

Rachel had nothing, just stared.

'This,' the colonel said, and pulled something from his jacket pocket and handed it to her. It was a beige beret adorned with a badge in the shape of a winged dagger.

Rachel turned the beret over in her hands, traced a finger around the badge. 'But this is ...'

'I know exactly what it is, corporal, and so do you.'

'You mean ...'

A nod from the colonel. 'The padre you just saw go

through those goons in there like an RPG through a bale of straw? He's SAS.'

ALEX ARRIVED home shortly after one in the morning. He was too tired to stay up but too awake to go to bed, so he poured himself a drink and sunk down into his sofa in the dark, tossing the contents of his glass into the back of his throat. There was no burn, just a pale warmth and a chance to stay numb a little longer and stall the arrival of tomorrow.

He ached everywhere and it was a pain he enjoyed. The fight had been easy, too easy, really. Yes it had got a little interesting at the end with the shotgun, but nothing he couldn't handle. He couldn't really remember the ins and outs of how he'd got into the world of illegal underground fighting, but once there it had given him the stress release he'd been searching for, a way to rid his soul of the anger and the aggression which bubbled up inside him relentlessly. It was certainly more effective than going to see a counsellor. And prayer had solved nothing. Alex was still pretty sure God was listening – that was what faith was all about – it was just that he could've done with a few answers instead of the stony silence from Heaven's one and only. He remembered that a lecturer had once told him during his theological training that sometimes we must look for God's answers in his silence. It had sounded wise and deep at the time, but now those words rang hollow. Alex didn't want silence. He wanted God's voice. He wanted to hear it, like the first time it had come to him, clear and rich and just for him, and all in a moment when he'd been up to his waist in an inexplicable hell, facing off against the worst that evil had to throw at him. He'd been a soldier in combat, thought he'd seen everything and worse, but what he'd seen then still haunted him. What he'd done still haunted him. And the voice that had called him back to himself, to who he was and what he could be, that haunted him too. And he almost wished that it didn't, because the seeming absence of it now was the most unbearable pain, a hollow wanting that he could only deal with by shutting away, locking it deep down inside.

On the coffee table in front of him the piece of paper Colonel Blake had given him stared back at him in silence. Around it sat dozens of scattered photographs, actual real photographs, something he'd always prided himself on, rather than keeping everything 'in the Cloud'. The images were of moments that showed a happy Alex, a joyous Alex, an Alex he himself no longer recognised. He was staring at a stranger from a time when everything wasn't so complicated. It was one thing to be a soldier, but a padre? And not just any padre either, one who'd served in the SAS? Like oil and water those two things didn't mix; two parts of his personality, his very soul, forever destined to never be reconciled with each other: the warrior and the man of God.

Alex shook his head in an attempt to dislodge the confusion of thoughts buzzing his brain and went back to the folded piece of paper. He'd known the colonel was keeping tabs on him, but for him to turn up unannounced at a fight? And why had he brought that corporal with him? Alex knew the answer was on that piece of paper. He leaned forward, opened it, and started to read.

A phone rang.

Alex ignored it, his eyes flicking across the words in front of him, unable to take them in.

The phone rang again and Alex pulled it from his pocket and answered, knowing full well who it was.

'So, have you read it yet?'

'You know what time it is, right?' Alex said.

'Then you have read it.'

'I'm looking at it now.'

'Good,' Colonel Blake said, 'Then I'll see you in the morning.'

'It is the morning.'

'Exactly.'

Alone in the silence of his house, Alex reached for the bottle and poured himself another, this one even larger than the first.

CHAPTER ELEVEN

'You look like shit.'

Having arrived at the colonel's office barely a minute ago, Alex ignored the observation and, without waiting for an invitation, sat down.

'I like what you've done to the door,' Alex said, nodding back at the hole he'd spotted as soon as he'd arrived.

'It had an argument with that shepherd's crook of yours, and I've not got around to repairing it,' the colonel said, then added, 'I'm half tempted to make them general issue. Pretty lethal.'

Alex breathed deep, which made the colonel's office swim a little.

'I'd offer you coffee,' the colonel said, 'but your breath is already enough to cut through a bank vault.'

'Listen, Colonel,' Alex said, 'if you think I've come down here just so you can shower me with compliments, I'll head back home, thanks.'

Colonel Blake moved around to his own side of the desk and took a seat.

Alex leaned forward, resting his elbows on his knees,

fists clenched together, white-knuckle tight. He'd done his best to make himself presentable, but a shower and clean clothes could only do so much. He'd seen the bags under his eyes, wondered how skin could get that dark. He looked and felt like what was on his mind: death. Awake or asleep, it haunted him, and it wore the face of the men he'd killed to save that patrol, dressed in their clothes, would dance past him when he least expected it, a scent caught on the wind that would snap him in two with a memory that would send him running to the sink to puke. He'd killed other men, but they didn't haunt him, because all of that had been a part of the job. If you were going to pass selection and join the SAS you just had to accept that killing was going to be a part of what you would do. The exact opposite was true of becoming a padre, a job which was about saving people, not slotting them.

Colonel Blake made an attempt to look relaxed and went to speak but Alex cut in first. 'The hell is this about, Sir?'

For a moment, the colonel didn't move. Alex wasn't sure whether or not he was about to get his head chewed off, but there was something in the way the colonel was looking at him which made him realise something else was going on.

Colonel Blake eased open a drawer and removed an iPad. 'You read the corporal's testimony?'

Alex nodded.

'Good. Now, what I'm about to show you is highly confidential,' Colonel Blake said.

'When has it ever been anything else?'

The colonel, having tapped the screen a few times, placed it on his desk and spun it round so that whatever was on it was facing Alex.

Alex reached for the iPad. The screen showed a video file keyed up and ready to play.

'Before you watch that,' the colonel said, 'I need you to remember what I said last night, about needing you; soldier and padre, both parts. And right now, with this?' the colonel tapped the screen with the tip of a finger. 'I'm not entirely sure which part I need more.'

'My ego's too broken to be fixed,' Alex said.

'What about your faith?'

Alex almost laughed. 'At the risk of repeating myself, Sir, what the hell does this have to do with me?'

'What, apart from the fact that you served with Matt in the SAS?'

'That was a long time ago,' Alex said. 'If he needs someone to talk to, that I can do, but I don't quite get why you're being so, well, weird about what looks to me like nothing more than a job that went to shit.'

The colonel said nothing more so Alex looked down at the iPad and tapped 'play' ...

... MATT and his squad froze as the darkness around them erupted with screams cut to shreds by weapons' fire. Flashes from the discharged weapons broke the blackness. They could hear rounds thumping into rock, ricochets pinging off dangerously in all directions. Whatever was going on there was no way Matt was taking his men into the thick of it. Instead, he kept them all back, safe in the shadows, waiting for whatever was going on to play itself out.

Whatever was going on ...

Matt thought about that for a moment. He'd been in fire fights before. He'd been pinned down for over 48 hours, running out of rounds quicker than time, waiting to get over-run. He'd witnessed what an IED can do to someone and how little is left of them, after they've been turned to pink mist, when you're trying to pick up the pieces to send enough back home to their family to give them something to grieve over. He'd been shot, stabbed, blown up, and carried the scars – inside and out – to prove it. Hell was one thing he was used to. It wasn't home, but it was somewhere he knew better than most. But what he was hearing right now? It was like nothing he'd ever heard in his life. And that was saying something.

Silence came down like a wall. Matt's ears popped with the sudden pressure of it. 'Goffey: Now!'

Rich lobbed the flashbang. Matt and the others ducked down, eyes shut, ears covered. The thud of the explosion thumped them hard.

'FUCKING MOVE IT!'

Matt's command clicked the team into action. Switching on the high-powered lamps bolted to the picaninny rails on their weapons, they moved as one, racing down the last few yards of the tunnel and out into a cavern ready for a fire fight, expecting it. What they found waiting for them was an abattoir.

Matt, weapon in his shoulder, scanned the scene before them. The cavern itself was about the size of a small house. He could make out swirls on the walls from whatever river had created it however many thousands of years ago. He flipped the red filter off on his helmet to give him full beam and the others followed suit. He saw boulders from the roof, the size of cows, littering the floor, which didn't make him feel entirely easy about strolling in for a look-see. Water was dropping from the cave's roof, and that made no sense at all. The cave up to now had been bone dry. The local area outside was no different, no rain in weeks. So where was it coming from?

Matt wiped away some of the drops as they ran down his face, noticed that something wasn't right. The consistency ... it was sticky. And it smelled faintly of iron.

Matt looked up. Drops fell on to his face, stung his eyes.

'... Fuck ...'

It wasn't water. It was blood.

The cavern came into focus then and Matt looked over to his men to see the blood raining down on them all. It was a scene any self-respecting horror movie director would've been proud of.

'The fuck happened here, Boss?' Mick asked. 'Place is a slaughterhouse.'

Matt didn't reply. He was still taking it all in.

Moving slowly into the cavern, his footsteps dull echoes in the chamber, Matt knew something here wasn't right. The space was piled at the sides by crates, except for a stack of them which had clearly been dragged in a hurry to block up the only other exit from the cave bar the one they'd just entered through. That explained some of the sounds they'd heard earlier, Matt thought. But it didn't explain the blood. And he wasn't really sure what could. It was everywhere, as though someone had come in with buckets of the stuff and thrown it over every available surface. The walls were sprayed with it, not just part way up either, but high up on the roof as well.

'Here, boss,' Rich said. 'X-Rays.'

Matt walked over to the soldier and was joined by Steve and Mick. At Rich's feet were three dead men all in traditional Afghan dress, right down to the bandoliers of rounds hung from their shoulders and across their chests.

Each man, Matt was certain, was dead. That much was

obvious from the trauma the bodies had experienced, each looking like little more than lumps of meat torn apart by a dog, limbs hanging on by thin threads of moist flesh, heads stoved in, torsos torn open. But that didn't stop him taking a knee to check for a pulse. Always best to make sure. Nothing worse than having the dead wake up, realise they're not dead, then try to kill you.

'Wasting your time, Boss,' Steve said. 'That one looks like a lion got in here and had a good old munch down on his face.'

Matt knew Steve had a point, but he still went through the motions. Bad memories of having not checked properly still haunted him, but like all that he'd experienced out in theatre, he dealt with them like most everyone else he knew: he buried them deep. It also allowed him to check if their target was one of them. He wasn't.

Matt looked again at the bodies. They sure were fucked up to a truly unholy degree. Hell, even their heads had been torn open.

Matt went to go and have a look at the piled-up crates, but paused, looking back at the corpses. 'Lads, what do you make of this?' he asked and pointed at what was left of the insurgents' heads. Each skull had been cracked open and pulled apart, splitting it from their nose to the back of their head. To Matt, it looked like the left and right lobes of the brains had been neatly pulled apart.

'How do you mean, Sir?' Rich asked. 'They're fucked, right? What else do you need to know?'

Mick stepped forward and dropped down at Matt's side. 'You mean that?'

Matt nodded.

Mick pointed at each skull in turn.

'I'm not seeing it,' Steve said.

'Nope,' Rich said.

'The skulls haven't been crushed or hit with anything,' Mick said. 'These injuries aren't from a stray round.'

'So?' said Steve. 'They're dead. That's it. Fucked if I care, right?'

Matt glanced at Steve and Rich and pulled out his combat knife. 'The skulls have been split open,' he said, using his knife to point out what he was talking about. 'Pulled apart. It's like something was forced into them to prise them open.'

'Fuck. Right. Off.' Steve said. Then added, 'Boss.'

Matt continued. 'Only weapons we heard were AKs, right? They didn't do this. A round from one of those at the range they were firing at in here would take your head off.'

'So what's with all the crates?' Rich asked and moved away from the bodies to check on one. He knocked the clasps open and flipped the lid. 'Shit,' he said.

The others joined him, leaning in to have a look.

'Fuckers ...' Steve said.

The crate was full of weapons. And they weren't just thrown in, either. This was new kit. AR-15s, foam-packed. Matt could smell the gun oil; the weapons were slick with the stuff.

While Matt, Steve and Rich checked some of the other crates, Mick made a 360 of the cavern. When he got to the far corner he called for the others.

'It doesn't make sense,' Mick said, when they were all stood together. He was in front of the crates stacked up at the other exit. The pile wasn't neat, the crates clearly put up in a hurry. And then there was the blood. The crates had been painted in the stuff. It had soaked into the crates and was pooling on the floor. In the quiet, they could hear it dripping. The crates had been pushed in a little in the middle of the pile to reveal a gap barely large enough to allow a small child through. The edges of it were slick not just with blood but lumps of flesh, some stuck with cloth that looked like what the three dead X-Rays were wearing.

'Which bit doesn't make sense?' Rich asked, unable to peel his eyes away from the blood.

Mick stared at the crates in front of them. 'If these were piled up to keep something out,' he said, then nodded back over towards the bodies, 'then who or what did that?'

For a moment no one spoke.

Then Rich said, 'And where did all that blood come from?'

CHAPTER TWELVE

Alex hit pause on the iPad screen and sat back in his chair. 'What is this?' he asked.

'You tell me,' the colonel replied. 'I'll be forwarding this all to you, once we're done. So you'll have plenty of extra time to look at it in detail.'

Alex shook his head and sighed. He was in no mood for guessing games. Why wasn't the colonel just telling him what was going on?

'This has nothing to do with me,' Alex said. 'The only person, or people, you should be forwarding this to, is someone who can actually deal with it. Intelligence Corps, whoever, I don't really care. Just not me.'

'I can't,' the colonel said.

'Yes, you can!' Alex snapped back. 'Someone's hacked your emails, somehow got a hold of footage they shouldn't have, and the only thing required of you is to do the right thing and report it accordingly.'

Colonel Blake didn't move, didn't speak, just stared into the middle distance.

'Sir ...'

'No!' The colonel's voice was sharp and loud.

'Listen,' Alex began, but the colonel closed him down.

'No, you listen to me,' Colonel Blake said. 'This stuff has come to me from a source that knows something I haven't even thought about for over twenty years, something no one knows about, and something I'm not about to share with you right now, understand?'

Alex nodded, the colonel kept talking, regardless. 'What I'm asking you to do – I'm not making this an order – is to look into it for me, because I trust you and because I think you'll be able to help. Can you do that, Alex? Can you?'

Alex allowed them both a moment to just breathe in a little bit of quiet instead of filling it with words. It was clear that the colonel was on edge, more so than he'd ever seen him before. Perhaps he could, no should, help? Where was the harm in it? It would at least give him a chance to talk the colonel round to doing the right thing.

'Look, all I'm seeing is soldiers doing a recce of a cave system,' Alex said, 'flushing it out, nothing that warrants you getting me involved, never mind the fact that you've not told me why you're even involved in the first place. What's going on?'

Colonel Blake opened a large drawer to his left to remove a bottle and two glasses.

'Port?' Alex laughed, but the sound was cold and he heard no humour in it himself. 'It's not even ten o'clock!'

'It'll be more gentle on your stomach than the other stuff,' the colonel said. 'And as for the time, well, it's five o'clock somewhere, right?'

As he spoke, the colonel pulled the cork and poured out two generous measures.

Alex raised a hand to defer.

'Consider it medicinal,' the colonel said, insisting Alex

take the glass, passing it across with his left hand. 'Hair of the dog and all that.'

Alex took the glass, sniffed the thick, red liquid, then knocked it back. The port was warm and sweet and filled his mouth with the taste of raisins and cherry. It didn't make things better, but the feel of it was a distraction.

'Good, isn't it?' the colonel asked.

'It's port, Sir,' Alex said. 'It's never anything else. But I still don't see why I'm here, other than –'

The colonel raised an eye at Alex over the brim of his glass. 'Yes?'

Alex didn't answer immediately. It was a long time ago all of that, he thought to himself. How many years was it since he'd been in the Regiment? He couldn't remember, not with his brain still half pickled from the post-fight booze of the night before. But that didn't really matter. It was a small detail. As for the men he'd had the honour of serving with? Well, that was a different matter entirely.

Being in the SAS had been the best of times and the worst of times, Alex thought. Excitement, adventure, danger, derring-do, adrenaline, that's what people thought the Regiment was all about, glamorous even! Truth was, missions generally consisted of extended periods of crippling boredom interspersed with short bursts of even more crippling terror. And he'd lost count of the number of nights he'd spent hidden in a scrape in a bush shitting into a plastic bag to carry it back out again. It wasn't all abseiling down embassy walls to smash your way in through the windows and slot the bad guys. Glamorous? Nothing like. And not every trooper ended up as a best-selling author hiding behind a pseudonym, or on TV as the good-looking face of the British Army's Special Forces yelling at civilians attempting a piss poor version of Selection. God, that stuff was laughable!

'So this is about Matt, then?' Alex said eventually, squeezing back those memories to force them once again into a box in his mind he did his best to never open.

Colonel Blake nodded.

'It's years since I've seen him, Sir,' Alex said. 'We went our separate ways when I ...'

Alex's voice trailed off.

'Decided to train for the priesthood?'

Alex smiled. 'Not Catholic, not a priest,' he said. 'Church of England, Sir. Always was a sucker for tea and cake and a nice village fête.'

Colonel Blake laughed. 'You served together,' the colonel said. 'And there's a lot more weight to what that means in the SAS than other regiments. Can you remember the last time you saw him?'

Alex shook his head. 'It's years, that's for sure. We lost touch, and all this social media bollocks was never really 'Regiment', if you know what I mean, so it's just something that happened. I figured we'd bump into each other again, just not like this.'

'Fair enough,' the colonel said. 'I guess there's no such thing as a Facebook group for the SAS.'

'Quite,' Alex said.

For a moment or two, neither man said anything. What the colonel was thinking, Alex really wasn't sure. All he knew was that it was early morning, he'd watched part of a video put together from the helmet cams an SAS team had worn during a sweep of a cave system in Afghanistan, and that the one leading the team had been an old mate from his own time in the Regiment.

Colonel Blake leaned forward to rest his elbows on the

desk, hands clenched together. 'You need to watch the rest of it,' he said with a nod at the iPad. 'There's more. A great deal more, I'm afraid.'

Alex didn't like the tone of the colonel's voice. It betrayed something like fear, but there was more to it. Was it confusion? Disbelief?

'I'll come back later,' Alex said, rising from his seat. 'I'm knackered, Sir. I'll think better when I'm fresh.'

'Sit down!' the colonel commanded, his voice shifting decibels fast.

Alex did as ordered.

'Please,' the colonel said, obviously working hard to make his voice sound under control. 'Watch the rest. It'll make it easier later on.'

'Later on?' Alex said. 'Why? What's happening? First call is to find out who hacked into the system to find those files and send them to you.'

Colonel Blake went quiet for a moment. He picked up a framed photo from his desk, one of himself in his early army career, when he was all 'bravado and bollocks' as one of his sergeants used to say. He raised his eyes to meet Alex's stare.

'The files were sent anonymously. As for tomorrow, you're visiting Matt.'

Alex breathed hard through flared nostrils. 'They can't have been sent anonymously,' he said. 'Nothing would get through to your email account that wasn't already cleared. Security would see to that.'

The colonel raised his hands in submission. 'I'm just saying what happened,' he said. 'Came in last night while I was working late.'

'Then at the risk of repeating myself,' Alex said, 'send it to the right people who can sort it out. Even if it's not through absolutely official channels, you must know someone other than me who is qualified to look into this stuff, because it's not you and it's absolutely not me.'

The colonel set the photo back onto his desk. 'I've explained,' he said, 'and I can't do that. Not yet, anyway. I just need you to do this, and to trust me, Alex. Please. Just visit Matt. If that comes to nothing then, yes, I'll forward it as you suggest.'

It was clear to Alex that the colonel wasn't backing down. 'So you're organising my diary now, is that it?'

'I'm still your commanding officer,' the colonel said, his voice rising again. 'So if I want you to parachute into the middle of as terrorist training camp to perform a baptism dressed as the fucking Arch Bishop, then that's exactly what you will do! So yes, I'm organising your fucking diary!'

Alex wanted to go home. He wanted to be in bed. He wanted to curl up in the suffocating warmth and darkness of his duvet and never, ever come out again. But that just wasn't going to happen. The colonel clearly wasn't about to let this go.

Colonel Blake breathed himself calm and said, 'Watch the rest, Alex. Please.'

Alex went back to the iPad again and pressed 'play' ...

CHAPTER THIRTEEN

... STEVE KNELT AT THE FOOT OF THE CRATES, DIPPING A finger into the blood dripping down their surface, rubbing it between his hands as if to just make sure it was what they all knew it was.

'Saw a tank once,' he said, rubbing the dark red liquid between his fingers. 'There was this hole in the side, right? About as big as tennis ball.' He held his hands up to demonstrate, staring through a hole he made with fingers and thumbs. 'A shell had punched through nice and clean.' He rubbed his finger clean on his left knee then stood up. 'Other side, just the same, only in front of it, splashed across the ground, was all this red soup just everywhere. You see, the shell had punched right through, sucked all the air out.'

Mick and Rich turned to face Steve as he drew his story to a close.

'That vacuum? Just took the crew with it. Three blokes sucked out in less than a second through a hole no bigger than that.' Steve held up his right hand in a fist, put his mouth up against it, and made a loud, wet sucking sound.

Mick shook his head. 'Always with the happy stories, aren't you?'

Steve winked. 'Yeah, I'm fucking *Jackanory*, me,' he said. 'I should write novels like all those other ex-special forces wankers. I mean, how difficult can it be, right? Anyway, just reminded me of it, that's all. Never seen that much blood in my life until now.'

Matt stood back for a moment. They'd been sent here to find one person, an ISIL commander, and to bring him back for interrogation. So far they'd found three, all of them ripped to shreds, in a cavern that looked like a scene from a Hammer Horror film.

'Right lads,' he said, turning to his squad, 'we've still got a job to do.'

Matt reached out for one of the crates and lifted it out of the way. Steve, Rich and Mick joined in and they were soon staring down into darkness.

'Fuck me,' Rich said, staring at the hole before them. 'Get an eyeful of that ...'

Matt thought Rich had a point. The hole looked uninviting enough because they'd have to go in half crouched, but the slick of blood along the floor and splashed up the walls wasn't helping things.

'Whatever happened in here, the answer's down there,' he said. 'And so is our target.' Matt stepped through the gap in the crates before anyone could argue.

The cave was low and each man had to stoop, at times dropping to their knees to make it through. For Matt, his size didn't make things any easier, but he still pushed on, keen to pull the job to a conclusion as quickly as possible and to get the hell out.

After what seemed like an age of crawling and pulling their way through, the cave opened out again. Matt's lamp caught on something ahead. 'Contact!' he said, and each soldier raised their weapon.

The squad crept forwards until they were on what Matt had seen.

'Bollocks,' said Matt, staring down.

A body, most of its skin flayed off, was slumped on the floor at the edge of a large hole. Just like the others, its skull had been cracked open like an Easter egg.

'That's him, isn't it, Boss?' Rich said.

Matt nodded then caught something just off in the shadows. He swung his weapon round, the beam from the lamp on his helmet bringing into view what looked like badly folded clothing. But it wasn't clothing.

'They fuckin' skinned him,' Steve said, looking at what Matt had found. 'Some holiday this turned out to be.'

Matt, frustrated and confused by what they were finding, went to tell Steve to wind his neck in, but his voice was cut off by a high-pitched screech. The sound cut through him like a razor and he instinctively covered his ears, squeezing his eyes shut.

The sound stopped as quickly as it had started.

'The fuck was that?' Matt said.

No one answered.

'Sounded like a bat,' Mick said.

'Big fucking bat,' said Rich.

'Bite your fucking head off, man,' said Steve.

A scraping sound caught everyone's attention and they snapped round to see the body on the floor yanked into the hole in the floor.

'If it's all the same with you, Boss,' Rich said, staring at where the body had only a second ago been, 'I reckon we should fuck off sharpish.'

Another sound hit them then; two voices screaming in agony.

'I'm with Goffey,' Steve said.

'Makes two of us,' said Mick.

Matt made to move but as he did so something burst out of the hole in the floor. Everything went black, almost as though what light they had from their lamps had been sucked from existence. Then came the screech again and somewhere in it Matt heard a shocked yell.

'Wall!'

The blackness retreated, and Matt saw Rich and Mick race to the hole.

'Something took him, Boss!' Mick yelled. 'He's down there! The fucker took him down there!'

Matt edged towards the hole, the beam from his lamp creeping over the edge into the darkness. 'Wall? Wall!'

No response.

'Wall, answer for fucksake! Wall!'

A moan.

'What the fuck was that, Boss?' Rich asked.

'It just took him!' Mick said. 'I saw it! Just lifted him off his feet!'

Matt knew he had to get his men to focus otherwise he was going to lose them.

'The hole's not too deep,' he said. 'I'll climb down first. We get Steve then we're out. Understood?'

Mick and Rich didn't respond.

'I said, understood?'

Both soldiers nodded, but Rich muttered something as he did so.

'What is it, Goffey?'

'Nothing, Boss,' Rich said. 'Honest.'

'Like bollocks it is,' Matt said. 'Tell me.'

Rich glanced at Mick then back to Matt. 'It ... it looked like a bat, Boss,' he said. 'I'm not fucking joking, right? A fuck off massive bat ...'

'Then let's catch the fucker and take it back as a mascot!' Matt said and stepped down into the hole.

It was an easy climb, the hole small enough to allow Matt to brace himself against the sides as he climbed down and soon he was at the bottom. Mick and Rich weren't long behind.

Together they scanned the area they were now in. It was another cavern, only this one was pierced by a thin shard of light slicing into the darkness to stab into the ground just ahead of them. Matt could see that the light was bouncing off something on the ground but couldn't make out what. From where he was it looked like a smooth-sided rock sticking up to a height of about four or five feet. He made to walk over when a call came from Mick.

Matt raced over to find Mick and Rich with Steve. He was slumped up against a rock, his face was beaten up, and one of his arms was hanging wrong – broken, Matt knew immediately – but he was alive.

'You look like shit,' Matt said. 'Can you walk?'

Steve nodded and said, 'If there's a beer at the end of it, I'd pull myself there by my teeth.'

Matt ordered Mick to sort Steve out while he and Rich had another look at the cavern. There were two missing X-Rays and regardless of what Mick said he'd seen, he didn't think a giant bat was about to swoop at them.

Covering each other, they made a sweep of the cavern, finding no sign of the two missing insurgents. With no place left to look, Matt wandered over to what he'd seen cast in the light from the crack in the roof far above.

To Matt's surprise it was a huge clay pot, the lid lying broken on the floor.

Rich joined him.

'That's a bit Indiana Jones,' Rich said and leaned over to peer inside. 'Fuck me!'

Matt grabbed Rich and yanked him back raising his weapon to point it at the pot. 'What? What did you see?'

For a moment, Rich said nothing, just stared at the jar, mouth agape.

'Goffey?' Matt said. 'Talk to me: what did you see? What the fuck is in there?'

Matt was ready to empty a magazine into the jar if there was even a hint of something leaping – or flying – out of it.

'Bones,' Rich said at last, his voice unusually quiet. 'Some poor fucker died in there, Boss. Have a look for yourself. Fucking fuck ...'

Matt edged into the light, past Rich and towards the pot. He noticed then that the surface of it was covered in strange symbols and what he guessed was some form of writing. Peering over the lip he saw at the bottom, wrapped in chains, a skeleton so small it had to be that of a child. It was black with ash as though it had been burned.

'Who the fuck wraps someone in chains, drops him in a pot, and sets them on fire?' Rich asked.

'A kid,' Matt said, barely able to take in what he'd just seen. 'A fucking kid ...'

Footsteps caught Matt's attention and he turned to see Steve and Mick closing in on them. Steve was bloodied and his arm was now strapped against his body.

'We're good to go, Boss,' Mick said.

'Yeah,' said Steve and nodding at the clay pot added, 'No time for antique shopping.'

A smile broke its way onto Matt's face. The mission had

gone to shit. It was down to someone else now to figure out how everything had gone so quickly south. His job was to get them out. 'Reckon you can scramble up the hole?'

'I'd climb up an elephant's arse to get out of here, Boss,' Steve said.

Everyone laughed, but they were cut off as once again the high-pitched screech pierced the moment.

'Anyone got eyes on?' Matt asked as they all swept the cavern with their weapons, Steve now reduced to his sidearm.

Then something swept out of the darkness, piled into them with the force of a freight train, and blood danced in the air with their cries.

CHAPTER FOURTEEN

IT WAS EARLY IN THE AFTERNOON, AFTER THE STRANGE morning spent in the colonel's office, and Alex was drenched in sweat. With everything he'd heard from the colonel, from Corporal Coates' witness testimony, and seen on the iPad screen, he'd decided a workout was in order. And now, with his breath back, Alex flicked through his Spotify list and slammed on something mean and nasty. Fists up, he went into the heavy bag once again, chasing away the pain from the fight of the night before.

The garage was empty except for a recycling box overflowing with empty bottles of booze, a weight bench against one wall and, hanging from the ceiling, a punch bag. It was the heavy kind, big enough and tough enough to take anything you could ever want to throw, punch, elbow, kick and head butt at it. Puncture wounds from knife attacks the warranty absolutely didn't cover had been taped up. A single bare bulb lit the space giving it the air of a backstreet fight club. The air was cool and musty, the smell of sweat mingling in the air with the faint hint of dampness and mould.

Time stopped. All Alex could see was the bag in front of him. What he was doing wasn't fancy, never had been, but it was effective. Basher had found that out all too well the night before. Round house kicks and all that other stuff were only good for the movies and the occasional lucky break in a UFC cage fight. It was a bit different in close quarters, out of ammo, fighting in the skeletal remains of a house shelled to shit, grabbing anything to hand to take the other person down.

Knees and elbows held the power and there was less risk of damage. Mix it up with fists and a head butt and Alex knew exactly how to do serious damage, hard and fast. If the bag had been a person, his attack would have been devastating. As it was, the only blood showing was his own. He'd foregone the usual gloves, wanting to feel the pain, his knuckles skinned raw, elbows grazed. And still he kept on in at it, his mind fast-forwarding through what he'd seen happen to his old friend, Matt, someone he'd last seen back in his days in the SAS. Back before he'd heard the whisper-quiet, earth-shattering voice of God.

That last thought hooked right down into Alex's gut and wrenched out of him such a roar of hot anger that he stumbled. He tried to grab the heavy bag but he'd already lost his balance and landed hard on the garage floor. Rolling onto his back, he closed his eyes, focused on getting his breath back, the pain from his injured knuckles and elbows nothing compared to the pain he felt way down deep inside his soul.

The rattling trill of his front doorbell forced Alex to sit up, bitterness in his mouth, vomit clawing its way up his throat. The heavy bag swung ominously in front of his face and he swallowed hard. The bell rang again so Alex heaved himself up from the floor, made his way through the back door of his garage into the house, and on towards the front door. He stopped on the way in the kitchen to run his wounds under some water, dried them, then left them to the air rather than bandaging them.

The bell rang again as Alex pulled open the door and came eye to eye with someone he didn't want to see.

'Corporal Coates,' Alex said.

The corporal was in uniform, the multi-terrain pattern, or MTP, clothing doing little to camouflage the irritation in her eyes as she stared at Alex.

'Do I call you Padre or Sir?' Rachel asked.

Alex ignored the question and asked his own: 'Why are you here?'

'Because Colonel Blake ordered me to be,' Rachel replied, not even trying to hide her annoyance. 'I'm coming with you to see Matt.'

Alex sighed. He couldn't be bothered to argue. 'We don't even know if he's at home,' he said.

'We do and he isn't,' Rachel said, pulling out her phone and punching something up on the screen. 'He's here.'

Alex glanced down to see a red pin on a map. 'And where's that exactly?'

'Military hospital,' Rachel said.

'Can't be,' Alex said. 'Last one closed in '95, as I'm sure you, being a medic, would know. MOD has units embedded in civilian hospitals now.'

'We both know that,' Rachel said, dropping her phone into a jacket pocket. 'We also both know that the MOD has more than enough land to hide a few secrets from the public eye. Including this apparently top-secret medical facility which I only found out about earlier today. And I'd appreciate it if you didn't focus on the fact that I just used the phrase top secret.'

'Seems like Colonel Blake is just full of surprises, isn't he?' Alex said.

Rachel said nothing, just turned, and headed towards her car, a Subaru Impreza in matt black.

'I'll be five minutes,' Alex said, calling after Rachel. 'Need to shower and change.'

The only answer he got was Rachel yanking open the driver's door of her car to thump down into the driver's seat.

GREY CLOUDS WERE GATHERING, Alex noticed, pulling his front door shut. He wasn't one for reading into things too much, but the weather seemed fitting. Then the sun burst through and cut a swathe of gold across the path leading up to his front door, a sword of light slicing the day in two. When, a few minutes later and showered, he clambered into Rachel's car he gave her an address.

'What's this?'

'Matt's address,' Alex said.

'I told you, he's not at home,' Rachel said. 'He's at the hospital.'

'His wife and kids are,' replied Alex. 'And that's where we're going first.'

'What, Hereford? But that's hours away and I've got –'

Alex interrupted. 'You've got a job to do and so have I,' he said. 'So what say we do it properly from the off?'

He hadn't meant to snap at the corporal but he hadn't warmed to her attitude from the moment they'd met. He wasn't questioning her professionalism, far from it. And he wasn't exactly happy himself about being pulled in by the colonel and ordered around. But this was about Matt, and if they were going to find out what had actually happened in those caves then they needed to do this properly.

Rachel went to speak but snapped her mouth shut and instead punched the address into her satnav before wheel-spinning them away from the kerb.

ALEX AND RACHEL arrived outside Matt's house with late afternoon breaking into early evening. The journey had been an awkward mix of uncomfortable silence, another read of the file from Blake, and music Alex hated. But it wasn't his car and it was obvious that Rachel was as happy to be involved with whatever the hell they were involved with as he was, so he kept quiet. At points he'd wanted to mention the speed they were doing, particularly the moment, only a few minutes into the journey, when they'd shot over the top of a hill and into a sharp bend to see just ahead a convoy of armoured vehicles from 5 Rifles crossing the road. Instead of slowing down, Rachel had sped up and zipped through the convoy with a toot of her horn while the lads in the convoy returned the toot with blasts from their own horns and a ragtag collection of mock salutes. But then Alex had had an inkling that the journey was going to be interesting from the moment he'd slipped into the passenger seat to see that the vehicle had bucket seats, parachute harnesses, a roll cage, fire extinguishers and numerous spinning dials, none of which came as standard. It was a car not so much built for speed as to rip roads to shreds and Rachel, Alex noted, really knew how to drive.

Leaving the folder on the passenger seat, Alex climbed out of Rachel's car feeling, he imagined, rather like a co-driver in a rally car after a race. He walked up to the front door, leaving Rachel to catch up. He wasn't quite sure what to make of her yet. She was as career minded as anyone he'd met and so far all he was seeing was the uniform. He half wondered if that was the main reason Colonel Blake had roped her in as well to whatever was going on with Matt; someone to keep him in check. But if they were going to work together, no matter how briefly, he needed to know the person underneath. He hoped meeting Matt's family would help that along a bit.

The day was still cloudy and rain was in the air. It promised gloom, the British weather doing what it did best. As Alex rang the door bell he noticed a horse shoe lying just to the left of the path. He reached down and picked it up as Rachel appeared alongside. 'What's that?' she asked.

Alex showed her the horse shoe and she took it from him, weighing it in her hands. 'Brings you good luck, right?'

'Me? Nah,' Alex said. 'I've never been superstitious.'

'Whereas wearing a cross and believing in an invisible sky fairy ...'

Alex held Rachel's eye for a moment, then took the horse shoe back, slipping it into his pocket. He could have happily waded into a discussion on philosophy and faith and belief, but not only did he not have the energy, the door had opened and stolen the moment.

The woman standing in the open door hadn't changed much in the years since Alex had last seen her. She was small, barely an inch over five foot, slim, and still had the look of a pixie about her, her deep brown hair pulled up into a scruffy ponytail to bounce around on top of her head. Two pairs of arms were wrapped around her legs.

'Alex?'

'Hi, Becky,' Alex said.

Before he could do or say anything else, Becky flung her arms around him. Alex eventually reciprocated, doing his best to make it all feel natural. Though it was clear from the look Rachel was giving him that it was anything but.

'It's okay, Becky,' Alex said, his instincts as a padre taking over and telling him he wasn't being hugged simply out of rediscovered friendship, but desperation.

The hug went on for longer than Alex expected and when Becky eventually pulled away he saw staring up at him eyes red and sore from crying.

Becky let go then stumbled backwards a little as she tried to make space for Alex and Rachel to squeeze through into the house. The two pairs of arms around her legs revealed themselves to be a boy and a girl.

'Twins?' Alex said as he stepped past the front door. 'This is Corporal Coates, by the way. Doesn't smile much and drives like a lunatic.'

Becky nodded as Rachel crouched down and held out a hand to the boy. 'Hi,' she said. 'Nice to meet you.'

'That's Henry and his sister is Scarlett,' Becky said, smiling at the children. 'Turn four in three months.'

The two children stared at Rachel and in both of them Alex saw Matt. Scarlett definitely had her father's eyes, but Henry, Alex thought, took after him the most. It was a little eerie to see the image of his friend looking back at him from behind the face of a child.

Henry hesitated for a moment then shook Rachel's hand. 'Do you like dens?'

Henry's question bounced around the hall like a lost bee before Rachel answered. 'Have you made one?'

'It's the best den ever!' Scarlett said, and quickly stepped forward and grabbed Rachel's hand to drag her towards the stairs.

Rachel paused, looked to Alex.

'If it's the best den ever, then you'd be mad to miss it,' Alex said.

Rachel nodded and Alex sensed that she understood: he

needed a few minutes alone with Becky and this was a great opportunity to have just that.

Rachel stood and said to Henry and Scarlett, 'Well, you'd best show me then, hadn't you?' And with that, the three of them headed upstairs, the twins dragging Rachel up behind them.

'It's about –' Alex began, but Becky cut him off.

'Matt?' she said .'I know. He tried to kill me ...'

CHAPTER FIFTEEN

The horror of Becky's words hung in the air, poisoning it, and Alex couldn't breathe. Matt tried to kill her? What the hell was she saying? Why would he do that? She had to be mistaken. Post Traumatic Stress Disorder did bad things to people, Alex thought, but Matt? He'd always been together enough to deal with what the job asked. Plus, he loved it. Soldiering was what he did. He knew nothing else and loved only his family more. He'd never harm any of them!

Alex wasn't given a chance to speak as Becky led them into the kitchen and started opening and shutting cupboards.

'I'll put the kettle on. Tea? I don't think I've got any biscuits, but I'll have a look. I can make a sandwich if you want? Will Rachel want one?'

Alex held up a hand to interrupt but Becky ignored him.

'What do you like: cheese, ham? The bread's wholemeal and I think I've got some salad. We've already eaten you see and there's not much in the cupboards and ...'

Becky's words tumbled over themselves and Alex could tell she was trying to pour them into the space where silence and awkwardness might take root.

'We're fine,' Alex said, not wanting to delay the discussion more than necessary. 'We ate on the way up. Pork pie and a packet of crisps.'

'The two main food groups, right?' Becky said.

Alex laughed as Becky handed him a mug of tea. From upstairs a faint tumble of laughter rolled down the stairs, most of it, he noticed, from Rachel.

'So what happened?' Alex asked.

'It's a long story,' Becky said. 'Happened a few days ago.' Becky leant up against the kitchen cupboards. She shrugged then and Alex saw her blink away tears. She looked exhausted. 'They took him away, you know? Military Police. And no one's called to tell me where he is or anything! Why would the army keep the whereabouts of my own husband a secret? It doesn't make sense!'

Alex had to agree; it didn't make sense. But he also suspected that there was a very good reason, perhaps numerous reasons, as to why Becky was being kept out of the loop. And because of that, he wasn't about to leap in and tell her that he knew where Matt was. No. He was here to dig a bit, to find out a bit more to the story beyond what he'd seen on the iPad and read in Rachel's witness testimony. That was all. Alex asked, 'You want to tell me about it?'

Becky sipped her tea, took a deep breath, glanced over the mug at Alex. 'Like I said, it's a long story.'

'Then you'd better get on with it,' Alex said.

'He came back from an OP,' Becky said, pushing hair from her face. 'Five or six months ago I think. I knew something was up but he wouldn't tell me anything. Never does. This fucking job, Alex!'

Alex let Becky's anger bubble out, giving her time to speak again.

'You did well to get out, you know?' Becky said. 'Should've listened to my mum. She always said marrying Matt was a stupid idea, that I wouldn't be marrying the man, I'd be marrying the Regiment.'

Alex couldn't disagree. The number of marriages torn apart by the pressure of the job was the unspoken casualty list the Regiment refused to deal with. The other one was the suicides and no one really knew which list was the longer. 'Did he say anything about the OP?' he asked, knowing the answer, but wanting to keep Becky talking.

Becky shook her head and let out a short, bitter laugh. 'Dealt with it in the usual way,' she said. 'Down the pub with the rest of the lads for beer and shouting, then back to me as though everything's fine. But it's not, is it, Alex? Nothing's fine about what he does, what you used to do alongside him! It was someone else told me that he'd lost the rest of his team. He didn't even tell me that!'

Alex couldn't disagree. No one talked about what they did. The SAS didn't excel at hugging things out, or in modern parlance, 'decompressing'. 'So he told you nothing at all?'

Silence from Becky. Just eyes staring pain at Alex. 'Like I said, he was the only survivor. That much I do know. But he refused to tell me what happened. Not a fucking thing.'

Time moves on, Alex thought, but soldiers don't change. The Army can do its best to give everyone the image that it's all touchy feely, but that was absolute bollocks and everyone knew it.

'So he was different when he came back from this one, then?' Alex asked. He was fishing, but he didn't want to give away that he already knew some of what had happened. He wanted to help, not make things worse. If Becky knew just how messed up what Matt had gone through truly was then he had a horrible feeling it would tip her over the edge. And she couldn't afford to do that, not with Henry and Scarlett around.

'You know Matt,' Becky said. 'Huge on the outside, small on the inside, right? But this time he was quieter. And he's been getting nightmares. Waking up screaming. Like the night when –' Becky's voice choked itself off with a cry that caught in her throat. Her left hand shot up to cover her mouth and she shook as the memory of whatever had happened raked through her.

Alex put down his tea. 'Becky?'

Becky took a long, shuddering breath.

'Tell me what happened,' Alex said. 'But only if you feel that you can.'

Becky nodded, composed herself, then spoke. 'He'd been to a session with the army psych nurse or whoever she is,' Becky said. 'He always tries to get out of going, but then you all do, right?'

Alex didn't respond. It was funny how Becky referred to him as though he was still in the Regiment. But it was like the colonel said: no one ever really leaves.

'Anyway, he comes back from that and he's okay about it, you know? And he plays with the kids in the garden and we have tea and he seems good, like happy and relaxed. He puts them to bed, too, reading to them! You should've heard them laughing! He was reading Dr Seuss, doing all these weird voices the kids love. Makes them howl!'

Alex remembered Matt's laugh and smiled. It was good what he was hearing, he thought, all things considered. Whatever had happened to Matt and his team, and wherever Matt was right now, at least there were signs of hope in what Becky was telling him. Perhaps he'd be able to get all this sorted sharpish after all?

'We watched a bit of telly, had takeaway, then went to bed.' Becky stared past Alex and into the middle distance, her mind replaying the night before. 'He's not usually much into sex for a while when he comes back from an Op,' Becky said. 'It can be a few weeks before he's interested again. Does that sound odd?'

'Not really,' Alex said. 'Doing a job is hardly good for pillow talk.' It was something else the movies got wrong, Alex thought: tough soldiers back from duty taking their beautiful lady upstairs for a night of passion. More often than not, they were so exhausted, and so traumatised, by what they'd just done and experienced, that sex was the last thing on their minds.

Becky stayed quiet.

'It's okay,' Alex said. 'You don't have to tell me everything.'

Becky smiled but her eyes were all sadness. 'That night he was different,' Becky said. 'He was passionate. Rough, but not violent. It was like we'd just started going out or something, if that makes sense? He's not been like that in years. Neither of us have. I mean, marriage changes you, doesn't it? And the sex changes. But this? I don't know ...'

Alex had done plenty of marriage counselling as a padre. He'd just not been expecting to do it now. 'So, what happened then?' Alex asked, trying to keep Becky moving.

'We fell asleep,' she said. 'Properly, you know? Like wrapped up and safe. But then ...' Again, Becky's voice croaked and broke on her words.

'Becky?'

Becky's eyes flickered up at Alex. 'I woke up with his hands round my neck strangling me.'

CHAPTER SIXTEEN

Becky rubbed what Alex now saw were bruise marks just above the collar of her shirt. 'He was on top of me. Pushing me down into the bed. I couldn't … I couldn't breathe, couldn't move …'

Alex wasn't exactly surprised. Whereas Matt, he guessed, probably weighed in at 220lbs and could bench press a small car, Becky would have a job staying on her feet in a strong breeze.

'He was screaming!' Becky said.

Alex could see the horror of what had happened alive in her eyes as the memory of it etched pain into her words.

'I mean, like really screaming! And he was pushing down on me and I couldn't get out from under him and his eyes were … well, they were, I don't know, like it was someone or something else in there looking down at me, wanting to kill me! My own fucking husband trying to kill me!' A sob burst from Becky.

Alex had heard of soldiers with PTSD having nightmares, but he'd never dealt with anyone who had tried to kill his wife in her sleep. It was the kind of thing you saw on

TV as it added to the drama, but not so much in real life; it happened, but rarely.

'Was he saying anything?' Alex asked. 'While he was ...'

'Attacking me?' Becky said. 'Yes, but it made no sense. Kept on about being trapped and being free again and ... oh, I don't know, Alex. He was trying to kill me! I wasn't exactly taking notes!'

Becky took a breath, trying to suck in some calm. 'Some of the stuff he was saying, it was words but it wasn't. No, that sounds insane, but that's what it was. Like he was talking in another language but it was like no language I've ever heard.'

'Matt was never one for learning another language,' Alex said.

'Exactly,' Becky said. 'We went to France once and he couldn't even order a beer.'

'And you didn't recognise any of this other language?'

Becky shook her head.

Alex let a moment pass then asked, 'How did you get out? Did he wake up? Realise what he was doing?'

Becky shook her head. 'It was the twins,' she said, her voice breaking as she spoke. 'They must've heard what was happening. They were just standing at the door, Alex! Just standing there, staring at their dad trying to kill their mum! Can you imagine that? What the fuck kind of damage is that going to do to them?'

Kids were resilient, Alex thought, but something like this was going to have an effect, of that he was certain.

'Matt must've seen them,' Becky said. 'He froze, just stopped dead and stared at them. Then the next thing I know, he looks at me, tears streaming down his face, says sorry, and just leaves! He just fucking leaves!'

'He walked out?'

Becky nodded. 'Threw on some clothes and was out the door before I'd had a chance to get my breath back. I chased after him but all I caught was the tail lights of his car disappearing up the street.'

Alex remembered what Becky had said earlier about the Military Police. 'You said he was arrested?'

Becky wiped her eyes. 'That was after ...'

Alex wasn't expecting there to be more. Matt had attacked Becky, scared his kids, what else could've happened? 'After what?'

Becky stood up. 'I'll show you.'

Grabbing Alex's hand, Becky led him upstairs and to the main bedroom. Alex could hear Henry and Scarlett chatting along to Rachel in one of the bedrooms. He was impressed. Rachel had so far given nothing away other than her ability to snarl and look seriously pissed off. Clearly, there was more to her than being angry.

'The wardrobe,' Becky said, pointing. 'Behind it.'

Alex walked over to the wardrobe as Becky kept talking.

'It was when he'd gone that I noticed it, the blood ...'

Alex saw red smears on the wall disappearing behind the wardrobe.

'It was everywhere; on me, on the bed ...'

Alex grabbed the wardrobe to pull it away from the wall.

'I thought maybe Matt had cut himself, no idea on what, but that made sense, except there was so much of it and then I saw the marks on the wall, and ...'

Alex stared at the wall behind the wardrobe.

'What is it?' Becky said, stepping closer. 'I cleaned everything else, but this? I don't know, really, I just didn't want to touch it. I mean, it's weird, right? Gives me the shivers. That's why I just covered it up again.'

On the wall were symbols and what Alex took to be lettering, all of it painted in blood. Numbers, too, he realised, at first reading the sequence of six numbers like a grid reference, because that's what they reminded him of. Army training never leaves you and certain things just stick in your head so you see them without even realising. But why would it be a grid reference written in blood?

Alex pulled out his phone and took some photos. 'I'm assuming you don't recognise any of this?' Alex asked.

'Why would I?' Becky said.

'You wouldn't,' Alex said. 'But why would Matt do this? It makes no sense.'

'No shit,' Becky said. 'I called the Military Police, but I didn't show them this. I didn't know what he was going to do, if he'd totally flipped, was going to top himself, but if I'd shown them this they'd have just taken the piss.'

'They caught up with him?'

Becky shrugged then nodded. 'But I've heard nothing from him or the police, and that's not right is it? It can't be. Someone rang, told me he's okay, but that's it. Wouldn't answer my questions, tell me where he is, nothing!'

Alex heard footsteps and looked up to see Rachel now standing in the bedroom door. He quickly pushed the wardrobe back so that the children wouldn't get an eyeful of whatever was going on in blood on the wall.

'They're hiding,' Rachel said and looked at Becky. 'Said you had to go and find them. Something about a tickle monster?'

Becky's worried, broken face warmed suddenly at the mention of her children. And having met them only briefly, Alex could understand why. They were joyous, the pair of them, and it reminded him of something one of the tutors had said back when he was training for the church: a child's laugh was the only proof of God anyone should need. Alex wasn't quite so sure if faith and belief were that simplistic, but it was a cosy thought at least.

Alex showed Rachel the photo on his phone screen of what was behind the wardrobe.

'Well, that's fucked up,' she said.

'One way of putting it,' Alex said.

Becky said, 'What am I supposed to say to Henry and Scarlett? They keep asking where their dad is and why there was so much noise. I don't know what to tell them.'

'Nothing more than you already have,' Rachel said, and Alex saw that despite her hard edge, there was a kinder side to her, and he could see how both together would make her a medic you'd want treating you if things went south.

'They seem okay at the moment, right?' Rachel continued, 'and it's not like their dad has a normal job. He's had to head off in the middle of the night before hasn't he? That's all part of the job. So hopefully they'll soon forget what they saw.'

'You think so?'

'Absolutely,' Rachel said.

'And let us worry about Matt, okay?' Alex added.

'You know something, don't you?' Becky said, her eyes narrowing in on Alex, staring with steel hardness.

Alex said nothing, just returned the stare. What he actually knew was bugger all, but he couldn't tell her that. He had no idea, really, why Colonel Blake was interested in Matt. Yes, the videos and what Coates had said in her witness testimony all pointed to something horrible and inexplicable happening, but that was war. It fed on violence, grew fat on death, but even if he couldn't see something in what Blake had shown him beyond war taking its toll, it was clear that the colonel could. It was also clear that the colonel wasn't telling him everything, that there was something hidden behind all of this which Alex couldn't see; a small part of him wanted to find out what it was.

'Well, answer me!'

Alex was snapped out of his thoughts by the anger in Becky's voice, but said nothing.

'He's my husband, Alex!'

Becky swung her left hand at Alex with such speed he only just managed to step out of the way. The force of it sent her spinning and he caught her before she fell to her knees.

'You have to trust me, Becky,' Alex said. 'I'll tell you more when I know more, okay? I promise.' Alex wasn't quite sure when he'd know more, or if he wanted to know more, but it was becoming abundantly clear that what the colonel had got him involved with wasn't going to be as easy to conclude as at first he'd hoped.

Becky shrugged out of Alex's hold. 'You already know more,' she said. 'And you're not telling me that, are you?'

Alex's silence was all he could offer because what he knew he didn't understand and sharing any of it with Becky would only serve to make things worse.

'Thought so,' said Becky then pulled open a drawer in the dresser next to the wardrobe and removed an old tobacco tin, mottled with rust and dented from use. She handed it to Alex.

'What's this?' Alex asked. He'd seen plenty of tins like it, having carried a few himself, generally stuffed with survival kit and emergency first aid.

'No idea,' Becky said. 'It was stuffed under his side of the mattress. I found it when I was changing the sheets earlier, to get rid of the blood.'

Alex opened the tin. Inside were what looked to be pieces of dried meat wrapped in cloth. He closed it again, puzzled, looked at Becky.

'Disgusting, isn't it?' Becky said. 'Why would he have that? What the hell is it?'

Alex had no answers, only more questions, and he knew that now was neither the time nor the place to start asking them. He stuffed the tin into his pocket and turned to Rachel. 'We'd best get going.'

Rachel nodded and turned for the stairs. Alex gave Becky his phone number then followed. Downstairs in the hall, Henry and Scarlett watched them walk up to the front door and open it.

'Are you going to help Daddy?' Scarlett asked.

'Yes, that's exactly what I'm going to do,' Alex said. 'I promise.'

When he climbed back into Rachel's car and waved to Becky and the two kids, Alex knew that he had absolutely no idea how he was going to keep it.

CHAPTER SEVENTEEN

It took just over two hours to arrive at the hospital. Rachel heaved the car off the main road and down a non-descript side road, which took them on a winding, twisting route down into a small valley and then finally to a dell hidden on all sides by forest thick with shadow. The grey of the day hadn't improved much and the darkness from the trees only added to the gloom.

Rachel parked in front of what looked to be little more than a small house set in a clearing in the woodland. At its side stood a double garage against which was stacked a large pile of wood. It didn't look exactly military, what with its little garden, winding path, and white gate.

'Thanks for the lift,' Alex said, unbuckling himself and wondering if his backside would ever be as numb again. 'When did you do the evasive driving course?'

He'd recognised Rachel's skills for exactly what they were: professional. She didn't drive like someone who was only in it for the speed. She drove with a skill and alertness achieved only by being taught by the best. Alex had done similar courses himself and used those skills to save his own life more times than he could remember.

'Last year,' Rachel said then nodded at the buildings in front of them. 'Doesn't exactly look like a hospital, does it?'

That's probably the point, Alex thought, shaking his head, half wishing Colonel Blake was here to explain himself and give him a very good reason as to why they were now standing in front of somewhere that they, he was pretty sure, shouldn't even know about, never mind know the location of.

They both climbed out of the car, Alex bringing with him the folder from Blake.

The front door to the house opened and out walked a man dressed in the same MTP clothing as Alex and Rachel. He approached them both with a stride dedicated to making sure everyone who saw it knew he walked with purpose. He was tall, Alex noted, and slim, and wore thin-rimmed glasses.

'Padre, Corporal,' the man said. 'I'm Major Tucker and I need you to leave immediately.'

'Not quite the welcome I was expecting,' Alex said and, reaching into his pocket to pull out the tin given to him by Becky, added, 'Colonel Blake sent us. He wants this analysed. It's relevant to your most recent patient, Matt Harrison, with whom we will need to have a little chat, if that's okay?'

Major Tucker opened the tin to look at the contents before his brain had time to catch up and refuse Alex's request.

'What is this?'

Alex said, 'We don't know, or we wouldn't be asking you, would we? You will only need a sample; leave the rest in the tin.'

'But these have haven't exactly been kept in a sterile condition,' the major said.

'Not important,' Alex said, knowing he was pushing his luck. 'You have someone here who can do this, correct?'

Alex needed to get control of this from the off, keep pushing, or else they'd fail before they'd even started. And sometimes the best approach was bullshit and bravado.

'Yes, well,' the major said, fumbling for words while pinching a sample from the tin with his fingers and then handing it back to Alex, 'but this doesn't mean I have to allow you to go any further, not least because I have no idea who Colonel Blake is.'

'Oh, I think you do,' Alex said, staring past the major and towards the house and slipping the tin back into his pocket. A small hand-painted sign on the gate said, Shady Glade Cottage. 'So can we get a move on, please?' He then added, with a nod towards the house, 'Nice name by the way.'

'Tucker or Shady Glade?' the major asked.

'I'm assuming you're stuck with one and that the other isn't simply to make people want to come here on holiday.'

The major said, 'The correct name for this place is Unit 69, but we don't use that, for obvious reasons.'

'Fair enough,' Alex said. 'Nothing says top secret more than an unnecessary sexual reference, right?'

The major glanced down into the tin and by the look on his face clearly wished that he hadn't. 'I'm not sure it's possible to have this analysed in less than 24 hours,' he said.

'Major, as I said, Colonel Blake will be expecting us to report back in the next hour,' Alex lied, 'about the contents of that tin and about your newest patient. This won't take long, I'm sure.'

The major was silent for a moment, using the time to

stare at Alex, then Rachel, then back to Alex. 'Your colonel rang some time ago,' the major said. 'Spoke to one of my staff. This is all a bit out of the ordinary if you don't mind me saying so.'

'I served with Matt,' Alex said. 'That's why I'm here. Corporal Coates is my medical adviser. To maintain a level of independence. I'm sure you understand.'

The major let out a short snort, turned on his heels and marched back towards the house.

'After you,' Alex said, turning to Rachel, but she was already stepping past him.

Once inside the house, and after the usual security checks, and some not so usual, Major Tucker led Alex and Rachel down a short hallway to a door which looked like it should've led them into a cosy lounge but instead placed them in a lift. No one said a word until the lift came to a stop after dropping for a few seconds.

'He's down here,' the major said, leading Alex and Rachel along a white corridor bright with light from bulbs set into the walls and running down the middle of the floor like a runway.

'Why was he sent here?' Rachel asked. 'And what exactly is "here" if you don't mind me asking, Sir?'

The major didn't answer Rachel's question and came to a stop outside a nondescript door. He handed Alex what looked like a key fob. 'Press this button if you need assistance,' the major said, 'and I'll come running.'

'Won't be necessary,' Alex said. 'Like I said, we're old friends.'

Rachel said, 'Major, you're making this sound like Matt is dangerous.'

The major didn't reply.

'Major,' Rachel said, 'is he dangerous or not?'

The major shook his head. 'He's shown no signs at all of being dangerous. In fact, he's been placid since his arrival.'

'So why is he in here then?' Rachel said, continuing her attack. 'You've not told us what this place is. Matt's wife doesn't even know where he is. What's so secret?'

The major slid a card into a slot above the door handle. A little red light at its side turned green. 'You said you served together,' the major said, his eyes on Alex. 'Did he ever show any interest in ancient religions, ancient artefacts, dead languages?'

Alex shook his head. 'Matt? He was only ever interested in getting the job done and getting home. Why?'

'You'll see,' the major said. He then gestured towards the door. 'Once inside you'll be able to enter the room when this door is locked behind you.' The major opened the door into a lit space barely bigger than a wardrobe. 'Remember,' he said, 'just press that button.'

Alex stepped through the door and Rachel followed. The major closed the door behind them.

'I hope you don't mind me saying, Padre,' Rachel said, her voice a whisper, 'but this is really fucking weird.'

Alex didn't disagree.

'We still don't know what this place is, what it's for, why Matt was brought here instead of just being taken to a normal facility. Oh and well done on spoofing our way into here. Where did you learn to be such a good bull shitter?'

Alex laughed and pressed a button marked 'open' on the wall in front of them. The second door opened a few seconds later with a *Star Trek* swish.

The room beyond was as homely as a secret military-run medical facility could be, comprising of wipe-clean floor, ceiling and walls, a bed, a sink, a metal mirror, two chairs, and a small table with some magazines. Set into the wall was a television showing something that involved good looking people attacking each other with swords. And it was the stark, clean normality of the room that made what was on the walls stand out even more.

'But this is the same as –' Rachel said.

'What we found behind Matt's wardrobe,' Alex said, finishing her sentence for her.

Wherever they looked, strange symbols and lettering in scribbled black ink stared back. Not in blood this time, which was a small grace at least. Alex quickly compared what they were seeing to the photo he'd taken back in Matt and Becky's room and it was identical. Even down to the six numbers in a row, looking once again like a grid reference, only this time they were different numbers. He quickly took a few snaps.

'Alright, mate!'

Alex pulled his eyes away from what was scrawled on the wall, put his phone away, and turned his focus instead on to the occupant in the room. Lying on the bed, and staring at them, was the man Alex had served with in the SAS and whom Rachel had last seen drenched in blood, carrying the remains of another soldier. He was reading a magazine about fitness. He looked over the top of his magazine and allowed his face to release a grin that could just as easily mean 'I'm going to kill you for fun' as 'good to see you'.

'Hello, Matt,' Alex said.

Matt said, 'It's been a long fucking time, pal. How's Jesus?'

'Oh, you know,' Alex said. 'Busy being the Messiah, hiring people like me to help people like you, that kind of thing. It was Colonel Blake sent me, though.'

'No idea who the fuck he is,' Matt said without looking up.

'Well for some reason he knows you,' Alex said, for a moment wondering again why, if Matt didn't know who Blake was, Blake had been sent the information on what had happened by the apparently anonymous source. That was something he'd be asking again later. It just didn't sit right.

Rachel said, 'What, no hugs from two old mates? Or don't you Special Forces types go in for public displays of emotion?'

Alex said, 'And this is Corporal Coates. You've met before, though you probably don't remember. Which is a shame, really, because she's a hoot.'

Matt dropped his magazine and stared at Rachel, brow furrowed deep. It gave Alex just enough time to take in what he was seeing and to ask himself exactly what he'd been expecting. The file in his hand, what the colonel had shown him, could not have been more removed from the man in front of him. Matt looked relaxed, healthy, no different really from the last time they'd seen each other, which was probably at least five years, Alex realised, if not more. He'd aged a little, clearly, with crow's feet deeply set at the corner of his eyes, but it was still Matt.

Matt sat up and his grin relaxed into a smile, though Alex could see that it was hiding something, as most smiles from anyone in the SAS did. And that wasn't always a good thing.

'Look, it's good to see you, mate,' Matt said, offering a hand, which Alex shook. 'You come to get me out of here?'

'Probably best if you tell me why you're here in the first place,' Alex said. 'And perhaps what all this is?' Alex gestured with a nod at the writing on the walls.

Matt jabbed a finger in the direction of the file in Alex's hands. 'I'm guessing that explains it all better than I could,' Matt said, then tapped his skull. 'Up here? Not a place you want to go poking around in for answers.'

'Just tell me what happened,' Alex said. 'Files never tell you everything. You know that as well as I do. What do you remember about the OP?'

Rachel moved from behind Alex to stand nearer the bed. 'I'm the medic who pulled you out of those caves,' she said. 'Full disclosure, I've no idea why any of us are here right now, though. So the sooner we crack on, the better, okay?'

Alex watched Matt move his attention to Rachel and his face turn dark, almost as though a shadow had slipped in behind his eyes. Then the shadow was gone just as quickly and Alex wondered if he'd imagined it. He was still pretty tired and more than a little sore from the evening before, so it wasn't really a surprise.

'Apparently I've got PTSD,' Matt said, an edge of sarcasm clipping the words. 'Who'd've thought, eh? An SAS trooper who's finding it a little difficult to deal with the shit he's gone through. I mean, that never happens, does it?'

Alex walked over to the two chairs and sat down. 'It does,' Alex said, 'but usually the only sign anyone gets of it is when the person in question ends up either slotting a mate with a souvenir weapon that only they know they've got, or throwing themselves out of a plane without a parachute.'

'You heard about Stacks, then?'

Alex nodded. Stacks had been a good soldier, born for it really, but then one weekend he'd gone skydiving only to unclip his rig at six thousand feet and hammer into the ground a few moments later to leave a smashed up corpse, a broken-hearted wife, and a hole in a field six-foot deep. The news had swept through the Regiment and Alex had raised a glass in private to a fallen friend.

'But why are you here?' Rachel asked, looking around the room. 'PTSD doesn't make this place make sense. Nothing does! The major told us nothing.'

Matt glanced at Alex. 'You been to see Becky?'

Alex nodded. He didn't need to say anything because he knew Matt wouldn't want to talk about it.

'And I guess you've seen the videos as well, right? The stuff shot from our helmet cams?'

'Yes,' said Alex, and could see from the look on Rachel's face that she hadn't. 'Trust me,' he said, before she had chance to ask, 'you don't want to see them.'

'I don't remember any of it,' Matt said. 'Not a fucking thing. My mind's a blank, like I was never even there. I've never blocked a job out in my life! Bits of them go missing, but that's what happens. You can't remember every detail of every fucker you've slotted and why, can you? But this? It's like there's nothing there. Not a fucking thing.'

Alex said, 'And you think that's why you're here?'

Matt shrugged. 'It's a secure facility,' he said. 'Someone somewhere obviously thinks I'm mad or bad or both.'

'Major says you're not dangerous,' Rachel said. 'So we still need a decent reason for you being here and us being sent to speak to you.'

Alex had a sense that there was more to it than what Matt was suggesting, then noticed a sudden change in the temperature in the room. At first, it was a chill, and he shuddered a little, only to find immediately after that the room seemed stuffy, as though he was in a kitchen and had just opened the oven door. There was even a faint sweet smell in the background of roasting meat. Maybe he was imagining it, hunger playing tricks on a tired mind, forcing it to focus on where his next meal was coming from.

Then Matt was on his feet and Alex hadn't even seen him move. 'They showed me the videos,' he said. 'My team were ripped apart! We were sent down into those caves on a snatch and grab, that much I do know, but what those recordings show? That's ... well, it's just impossible, isn't it? Something tore through us like a fucking whirlwind filled with teeth!'

'Sounds like everything went south fast,' Rachel said. 'Not your fault the intelligence was wrong, that there were more down there waiting for you.'

Matt laughed, but the sound was cold and hard. 'The INT was wrong? No shit!'

'How many were there?' Rachel asked.

Matt's lips curled his words into a snarl. 'How many? None is how many! None that was alive, anyway. The place was like a fucking horror movie!'

Alex stepped into the conversation, confused now by what Matt was saying. After what he'd seen from the helmet cams, the fire fight, the violence, Matt's team had clearly come up against enemy combatants. So, what the hell was Matt on about?

'I thought you said you couldn't remember?'

Matt paused, shook his head as though trying to dislodge something stuck inside. Then he winced. 'Shit ...' Matt dropped to his knees, swearing, his eyes squeezed tight shut.

Alex glanced at Rachel who was immediately on the floor next to Matt. 'Harrison? Harrison! What's wrong? Where's the pain? Have you experienced this before?'

Matt held up a hand. 'I'm ... I'm okay,' he said. 'Shit ... that was sore. Like someone stabbed me in the head!'

'Let's get you back to your bed,' Rachel said and went to help Matt to his feet.

'No.'

Alex looked down at his friend.

'No? Matt, what's going on?'

Matt, with controlled slowness, rose to his feet. 'I ... I remember ...' he said, rubbing his temples as though hit by a migraine. 'I remember it all ... Fuck ... I mean, how? What's going on?'

Alex rested a hand on Matt's shoulder. The smell of roast meat was stronger as well, and when he flicked a look across to Rachel, he saw her breath condensing in the air. Whatever was going on, whatever was happening with Matt, it was wrong, and in ways he couldn't explain.

'You said you couldn't remember any of it,' Alex then said, 'then you started telling us about what you found, how no one was alive.'

Matt nodded. 'It was a mess, mate,' he said. 'I mean, whatever was left of those poor bastards had been used to paint the walls!'

Alex said, 'You mean someone got to them first?'

Matt shook his head. 'Not who,' he said. 'What ...'

CHAPTER EIGHTEEN

Alex stood up, thinking it best to try and calm Matt down, when Matt snapped round to face him dead on.

Alex took a step back. Not because he was scared of Matt, imposing though he was, but because not a damned thing in that moment felt in any way right. None of it. Was someone outside of the room observing? There were hidden cameras, he was sure, but it felt more intense than that, not so much that they were being watched, but that someone had stepped into the room with them unannounced. And there was that temperature change again, cold then stuffy.

'I heard about Bonny,' Matt said.

The statement took Alex by the collar and choked him, because Matt couldn't have heard about Bonny, because he'd bought her as a puppy, watched her grow, and watch her die, and all in the years after they'd lost touch. News about the loss of someone in the Regiment spread pretty quickly, but news about the death of a pet? Not so much.

'Yeah,' Alex said, not sure what else to say, and absolutely sure he didn't want to talk about his dead dog. Didn't exactly seem all that appropriate. And in the time it had taken Alex to register what Matt had said, Matt had stepped closer towards him.

'Who's Bonny?' Rachel asked, but her words seemed distant and Alex didn't answer.

'And how about that crook, huh?' Matt said. 'Told you it would come in useful, didn't I? How did it feel, you know, skewering that fucker?'

Alex stared up into the face of his old friend working hard to give nothing away. Perhaps Matt did know about Bonny, he thought? He clearly knew about what had happened on that patrol, proving that confidential meant shit in the army.

'Listen, Matt,' Alex said, holding a hand up, hoping to calm Matt down enough to work out just what the hell had snapped in his brain to make him go off on such a tangent. 'I don't know what you've heard, but Corporal Coates and I, we've been sent to talk to you about what happened in those caves ...'

Matt didn't answer. Instead, he said: 'Northcutt wants a word.'

The statement stunned Alex into silence. All he could do was stare up at the big man in front of him.

'He's here,' Matt said, his eyes growing wide as he stepped closer still, forcing Alex back, his legs knocking into a chair. Matt tapped his chest, then his head. 'He's in here!' he said. 'With me! They all are. We all are. And we've been waiting for you.'

Rachel stepped past Matt and stood between him and Alex. 'I think we should leave,' she said, then looked up at Matt and said, 'and I think you need to get back to your bed. I'll call a doctor.'

Rachel put her hand out towards Alex, signalling for him to give her the fob that Major Tucker had handed to them, when Matt back-handed her so hard she did a full three-sixty before landing on the small table, crushing it beneath her.

Alex stood motionless, staring down at Rachel's unconscious body at his feet, half convinced he was having an out-of-body experience, because this, right now, it made no sense at all, and hadn't from the moment the colonel had appeared at the fight the night before.

'Alright, Padre?'

The voice snapped Alex into the now quicker than a shot of adrenaline: it was Northcutt. Except that it couldn't be, because Northcutt was months dead; a soldier without a face buried under a flag and at the feet of his shattered family.

'I don't know what you're doing or how you're doing it,' Alex said, 'but I need you to stop, Matt. Right now.'

Matt's face broke its rugged features across a misplaced, mean-as-you-fucking-like grin.

'Why'd you let him kill me? Why didn't you save me like the others? Isn't that what you're supposed to do?' The voice was Northcutt's but it was coming out of the mouth of a man who'd never even met the soldier, at least Alex couldn't see how Matt ever could have. So how was he doing it? How the hell was this man, this old friend, speaking like Northcutt, who'd been dead for months?

'Told you, didn't I?' Matt said, his own voice back now. 'And like I said, he's not the only one ...'

'You need to stop,' Alex said, working to pull himself together again, seeing that Rachel was at last heaving herself off the floor and onto her knees, shaking her head as she came to her senses.

'Come on, Padre!' Matt said, except it wasn't Matt, it

was Northcutt again. 'Explain yourself. Tell me why you couldn't save me, why you couldn't do your job!'

Alex held up his hands, hoping to somehow get control of the situation. 'Matt ...'

The big man took a step closer and at last Alex's fighter instincts took over, both hands were up, and he pushed Matt back towards the bed. 'Back away, Matt! Back away!'

As Matt fell against the bed, Alex helped Rachel back onto her feet then pressed the button on the key fob.

'The fuck is wrong with him?' Rachel said, wiping blood from a cut above her eye.

'You all right?'

'I will be once we get away from your so called fuckup of an old friend,' Rachel said. 'Interesting reunion. Next time, make sure I'm not invited, okay?'

Alex turned them both towards the door but no sooner had he done so than Matt was in front of them, blocking the way. 'You've got something of mine, mate, and I want it. I'm hungry ...'

Alex had no idea what Matt was talking about. 'Get out of the way, Matt ...'

'I need to feed!' With a speed bordering on impossible, Matt grabbed Alex's coat pocket, the one holding the tin Becky had given him.

'Give it to me!' Matt roared, but Alex heard more than a voice in the words; there was an echo to it, as though Matt was yelling from the bottom of a mine, or during a storm, or in the middle of an earthquake, or all of that and more.

Matt's hand was in Alex's pocket. 'Where is it?' Matt said, his voice a rumbling growl of violence. 'It was here. I can smell it! What have you done with it?'

Alex grabbed Matt's wrist to yank him away when Matt roared in agony. He stumbled away from Alex, holding his hand out in front of him. To Alex's astonishment, Matt's hand was scorched black as though burned to charcoal, smoke rising from it in swirls.

Rachel stared wide-eyed at Matt's hands. 'What the holy fuck ...?'

Alex ignored her, dragged his eyes away from Matt's hand, and brought his open left hand down hard on the side of the soldier's head, slapping the flesh of his palm down hard against his right ear. Matt dropped like his leg bones had just vaporised, landing hard.

Alex pressed the button again on the fob, hard enough he thought to snap it in half. A moment later he heard a noise at the door. It quickly turned into frustrated knocking and muffled swearing.

Matt's smile broke into a laugh. And with it came a smell that made Alex gag, the roast meat now turned to a rancid, rotting stench, and the temperature in the room not cold anymore, but hot to the point of uncomfortable.

'The fuck is that?' Rachel said, covering her mouth and nose with her hands as the reek assaulted her.

The knocking at the door had turned to banging now, the muffled voices to shouts.

Matt pushed himself from off the floor, and as he moved closer seemed to grow larger, though that was impossible, Alex thought, but then so was the voice, the temperature change, the smell. And what had happened to Matt's hand.

Alex did a double-take: Matt's hand was healed! Where his arm had ended in charred, blackened skin, a fleshy hand could be seen. No wound, no burning, nothing.

The door to the room burst inwards and in rushed six bodies, five of which were onto Matt in a beat and had him on the ground, belly down. He didn't even struggle, Alex noticed, just kept his eyes looking not just at him, but into him. The sixth body was Major Tucker.

'With me!' Tucker ordered. 'Now!' Tucker grabbed Alex and Rachel and pushed them out of the room. As the door shut behind them, Alex heard Northcutt's voice one last time calling out his name and the sound of it tore a fresh hole raw and deep in his soul.

Outside, and still reeling from what had just happened, Alex waited for an answer from Major Tucker. None came.

'You need to leave,' the major said. 'Immediately. You should never have even been here in the first place. How the hell Colonel Blake knew to send you here after Matt ...'

'We're not leaving until you tell us what's going on,' Alex said. 'None of that was normal or PTSD or whatever the hell else you're about to try and convince us it is. And what about all that writing on the wall? Is that why you asked if Matt had an interest in dead languages? And while we're on the subject, how did he write it on the walls? No way he has access to a pen!'

'That isn't happening,' the major said. 'To be frank, that you came here at all is a surprise. Whatever it is that Colonel Blake knows, and whatever he's told you, I suggest you forget. As to the writing? Matt took advantage of a member of staff's poor personal admin and nabbed a pen that shouldn't have been in a pocket in the first place.'

'Lucky it wasn't used as a weapon,' Rachel said.

The major turned back towards the cottage only to be followed by Rachel. 'Major?' the corporal called out. 'Major! Wait! What happened in there? Do you know what is wrong with that soldier?'

The major spun on his heels and in the same movement pulled a Glock 17 from a holster and had it in Rachel's face. 'No, corporal,' the major said. 'I do not. That you know anything about this at all is worrying, so as I've just said, please forget it. All of it.'

Corporal Coates stared down the black, angular barrel of the weapon in the major's hand. 'None of this makes sense, Sir! What's wrong with that soldier?' She switched her stare to Alex. 'And what the fuck happened to his hand? You saw that, too, right? I'm not making it up?'

Alex shook his head, slipped his hand into his jacket pocket and pulled out not only the tin but also the horseshoe.

'No, we both saw it,' he said, staring at the curved piece of metal in his hand. The horseshoe was warm – no hot – to the touch.

The major said, 'You need to leave!'

'We are,' Alex said, replacing the horse shoe back in his pocket. 'Once you've told me what your folks found in that tin I gave you.'

Major Tucker holstered his pistol. 'Pineal glands,' he said. 'Half a dozen of them. And unless your colonel can call me before today is over and explain why you have them, then I'll be left little choice but to report it to the police.' And with that the major turned on his heels and was gone, the door to the cottage slamming shut behind him.

Rachel returned to her car, her pace close to a jog. Before Alex was able to say anything, she was on her phone. 'Colonel? Yes, it's Corporal Coates ...'

What followed was, as far as Alex could tell, a conversation that did not go the way Rachel wanted it to. And when it was over barely a minute later Alex thought that the rage in the corporal's eyes looked hot enough to scorch the ground.

'None the wiser?'

Rachel thrust her phone into a pocket. 'Get in,' she said.

'We're heading back and then that's me out of whatever short-lived idiocy this is and back into my normal life. I'd like to say it's been fun, but you know what? It's been the exact fucking opposite.' Rachel didn't give Alex a chance to reply and instead just climbed into her car and kicked the engine into life.

It was at that exact same moment that the front door of the cottage burst outwards, the shattered pieces of wood and brick and glass scattering like a hail of arrows, and Major Tucker's body launched from the darkness inside the building to land right beside Alex with a wet thud, the dead man's head shattering with the impact of an Easter egg hit with a mallet.

CHAPTER NINETEEN

INSTINCT TOOK OVER AND ALEX LEAPT OVER THE bonnet of the Impreza, shrapnel from whatever had just caused the explosion peppering the ground around him. Inside the car, Rachel had dropped herself across the front passenger seat.

Matt, drenched in blood, stepped outside into the fading afternoon light, and behind him came a black, doom-soaked orchestra of gibbering, yowling shadows.

The impossibility of what was happening caught in Alex's throat and hamstrung him all at once. He couldn't move, couldn't breathe. The howls and screams from the cottage were growing louder and with it rolled the stench Alex had noticed in Matt's room, only now it was as though an abattoir had opened its doors to the sun, the sweet, cloying stench of death dragging itself out on bleeding claws and into what remained of the day.

Alex heard the Impreza's engine kick into life with a violent growl followed by a screech of the vehicle's horn.

'Get the fuck inside!' yelled Rachel. 'Now!'

Alex jumped to his feet and made to move only to find

his left leg snagged on something, bringing him down sharp into the dirt, grit and glass snicking at the skin on his face, stabbing into his palms.

'I said get in!'

Alex was about to shout back but then caught sight of what had tripped him up. It wasn't a branch or a rock, but a hand and the grip on it was squeezing bright lights of pain into his left leg.

Alex kicked out with his right foot as another hand reached up and latched on, as the clearly dead, but now impossibly animated, corpse of Major Tucker held him down. A volley of kicks did the job of dislodging one of the dead hands, but the grip from the other was getting tighter and tighter. A moment later and the pain peaked, filling Alex's head with sparks, as the fingers found their way through cuts in his trousers and dug into his flesh, drawing blood.

The driver's door flew open as an angry and terrified Rachel leapt out. 'I said get in the –' The corporal's voice was cut in half when she saw exactly what was delaying Alex. However, the reaction he was expecting, which would involve screaming and terror, was not the one he got. Instead, the corporal, her face riven with both disgust and bemused fear, brought a foot down onto the dead arm of Major Tucker gripping Alex's leg, the bones cracking and popping loudly under the stomp. The hand reacted in the only way it could and the fingers sprang from the wounds they had inflicted on Alex's leg. Rachel reached down to pull Alex up. 'You okay?'

'Tickety-boo, thanks,' Alex said, as beside them the remains of Major Tucker rose to its feet.

Alex was now able to get a proper look at the hellish thing which had assaulted him. To all intents and purposes, it was all still there, just not in a way which agreed with any sense of known logic. The left foot was not only twisted round to face backwards, but was hanging on by a ripped slab of flesh, the weight of the body taken instead on the bones sticking out of the bottom of the leg to jab into the ground. Alex could not make out any part of the body which had not been touched by violence, clothing torn, skin shredded, broken bones lancing outwards through the meat of what had once been a man, yellowing marrow dripping from where their milky surface had been shattered. But it was the head which took the horror to a place Alex could not, even when faced with its blood-red reality, accept. He'd heard the skull shatter, but that didn't account for the mess facing him now. Hanging from the neck and down across the chest like a bib, was the dead major's face, a mask seemingly peeled off from the skull. The lips were moving, muttering obscenities, laughing. Where the neck and the head had been was a giant rose of revulsion, a bright and glistening mess of blood and teeth and brain and bone. An eye, somehow still attached to the optic nerve, hung loose and pendulous.

Corporal Coates turned away from Alex and heaved. A vibrant, steaming stream of vomit burst from her mouth and splattered Major Tucker's monstrous remains. Alex briefly wondered why he wasn't reacting in the same way, but knew it was because he'd seen worse. Warranted, the bodies he'd encountered during his life as a soldier had been dead, but when you'd seen what an IED could do to a foot patrol, or the heat inside a tank to the bodies of its trapped crew after being taken out by a shell or three, there wasn't much you couldn't stomach.

Alex pulled the corporal away from the dead major as a loud, wet clang forced them to drop line of sight with it to face another body flung from the cottage by Matt, this one having landed on top of the Impreza's roof with enough force to bend the door pillars and shatter the rear window.

Wiping her mouth, Rachel made to move towards the car when the body on top of it raised its smashed head, opened its shattered mouth, and roared.

Alex tapped the corporal's shoulder and pointed at the cottage. 'That doesn't look good,' he said, aware of the enormity of his understatement, at the same moment pulling out his mobile phone and booting up the camera.

Matt was now striding towards them and with him came a tumbling, churning mass of ravaged humanity.

'I'm not sure this is the kind of thing you should be putting up on Facebook,' Rachel said.

Alex filmed what was approaching them: bodies of soldiers and of doctors crawling over each other, each of them a testament to what awfulness could be enacted upon the human form and for it to still look 'human'. Legs broken and twisted and crushed, arms ripped in half, chests stove in or burst outwards, but it was the heads which really caught Alex's attention, because each of them looked as though they'd been sheared down the middle, either by an axe or another sharp implement, then pulled apart to hang open like giant clam shells, steaming gore pouring out from within.

The sound of Rachel slamming shut the boot of her car yanked Alex away from the vision of the approaching dead. In her hand was his crook and, with the leap of a gazelle, she was up and standing on the back of her car. Then, with a full body swing, she brought the head of the crook around with such speed that all Alex really saw was a blur followed by the dead thing on the roof tumbling through the air, what was left of its head flying skyward.

'You brought my crook?' Alex said, slipping his phone back into a pocket.

'Blake gave it to me,' Rachel said. 'Told me to give it to you when the moment seemed right. I'm thinking this is that moment.'

Rachel tossed the crook to Alex and jumped down next to him, landing as he caught the steel bar in his hand.

'Effective, isn't it?' he said.

They both stole a glance at the advancing mass of ravenous dead.

'Against one or two, yes,' Rachel said. 'But against that?' The corporal shook her head. 'Which reminds me,' she said, 'when this is over, I need you to explain to me what turned an SAS trooper into a Jesus freak.'

'It's a long story,' Alex said and moved. A few strides and he was back around the passenger side and this time managed to get into the car before anything bad happened. Rachel jumped in next to him. The engine was still running and the corporal clicked the gear lever into first and hammered her right foot to the floor.

The car took off at a pace that threw Alex back into his seat. Scrambling to thread himself into the harness, he instinctively ducked as he saw through his window Matt heave another body towards them, then another, the animated corpses landing around them like mortar rounds, bursting on impact to send clouds of dust and blood into the air. But it was clear nothing was going to stop Rachel now that she was behind the wheel, and they sped onwards, away from the cottage, away from his old Regiment mate, and away from whatever gate of Hell had just been opened to allow what they had both just witnessed to spew forth.

'Jesus Christ ...' Alex muttered, the words sounding like

he was swearing, but deep down, he knew that they were a prayer, brief, desperate and raw.

Ahead the road was black and wet, the sky turning to a broiling mass of angry clouds, as a storm raced overhead and swallowed them up.

CHAPTER TWENTY

COLONEL BLAKE'S FACE WAS AS DARK AS THE STORM that still angered the night sky and which had not at any point relented in chasing Alex and Rachel all the way back to base.

'This is my home, Carter, you know better than –'

Alex ignored the colonel and stepped over the threshold of the front door and into the hallway, gently but firmly pushing the man to one side with his crook. Corporal Coates was a step behind him.

'Whoever it is, tell them to royally bugger off!' came a female voice from somewhere deeper in the house. 'And bring me another gin!'

The colonel stood staring at Alex and Rachel, his hand on the handle of the still open door, then his nose curled and he held a hand up to his face to cover it.

'What in the hell ...?'

'Exactly that,' Alex said, 'because Hell is the only thing which has even the slimmest of chances at explaining what we've just witnessed, Colonel. Unless you can tell us different. And I hope you can. Or maybe I don't, because I'm not sure any explanation or reason is going to make any of this better.'

'It's nearly midnight.'

'I don't care if it's nearly time for your once-a-month get lucky with Mrs Blake,' Alex said. 'We've just spent most of today either driving between here, Hereford and some place that shouldn't exist, being attacked by someone I once called a friend, or trying to get the hell away from, well I don't know what from, because what I think it is, well that's just impossible. We need to talk. And now!'

Alex watched the colonel's eyes narrow and could see that his words had potentially hit closer to home than he'd aimed for, but if they had the desired effect, all the better. It had been a rollercoaster of crazy since the colonel had shared with him the details of Matt's OP, and what Alex needed right now was answers. He wanted this to make sense, to be explained away by something tangible, because the answers being thrown at him by what had happened so far were little more than a trip into insanity. The answers were probably hideous and violent, and most probably either illegal, or at the very least, one of GCHQ's best kept secrets, but they needed to be real. What they couldn't be, what he absolutely couldn't be dealing with right now, was the evidence pointing to something else, something leaning less towards the real and more towards the darkly ethereal.

The colonel shut the door and to Alex it seemed to take rather too much effort to do so, not because the door was thick and heavy, but because the night didn't want to be shut out.

'In there,' the colonel said with a nod to a door on the left. 'I'll be back in five.'

Alex led Rachel through the door and into the room on the other side, flicking the light on as they entered.

'Bloody hell,' Rachel said. 'It's like walking onto an episode of *Antiques Roadshow*.'

The room was small, not so much because it was built that way, but because of how it was furnished. A tatty sofa and armchair sat atop a worn rug surrounded by a treasure trove of knick-knacks Alex assumed to be on the more expensive side of collectables. Shelves groaned under the weight of vases, candle sticks and ornaments. What wall space there was, was a patchwork quilt of pictures, both painted and photographed, jostling for position.

'This is what happens when you have too much money,' Alex said, picking up a bowl inside which was a small piece of card inscribed with the words, 'Roman pot, 110 AD.'

A snuffling, swishing sound entered the room, followed by a soft, 'Woof.'

'And this is Reggie,' Alex said, as the colonel's massive, chocolate-brown, dog sauntered into the room to roll onto its back at Alex's feet. The thump of his tail on the floor was the sound of thick rope on wet wood.

'That's not a dog, that's a wolf,' Rachel said.

Alex crouched down next to the animal and scratched its upturned belly as Colonel Blake entered the room, easing the door shut behind him.

'Let's make this quick,' said the colonel.

Alex rose from his feet to stare into the eyes of his commanding officer. 'No,' Alex said. 'Let's make this honest.'

The colonel stood his ground against Alex's stare. 'And what's that supposed to mean?'

Alex raised his phone for the colonel to see the screen and played back what he'd filmed earlier. The screams and howls filled the small room and Alex watched the colour drain from the colonel's face until, when the short video stopped, and the man had sat down in the armchair, his face was as grey and damp as a gravestone in the rain.

'What ... but that's ... no ...' the colonel muttered, his voice dashed into splinters by what he'd just seen, horror raking his face into lines, draining it of all colour.

'And there's this,' Alex said, flicking now to the photos of what had been found on the wall behind the wardrobe at Becky and Matt's house, and on the walls of Matt's hospital room. 'Recognise it?'

The colonel shook his head.

'Well, you should,' Alex said.

Rachel said, 'You mean you've seen it before?'

'Yes,' Alex said, 'in the footage from the helmet cams. It was on the walls of the cave Matt's team were in. I knew I'd seen it somewhere else.' Alex eased down into the sofa opposite the colonel. 'And finally this,' Alex said, and placed the tin on the table in front of them. 'Pineal glands, apparently, found by Becky under Matt's side of their bed. Six of them. I don't know what pineal glands are, Sir, but that there's six of them means there are six people who don't have them. And I'd put money on their removal from the human body being a little more involving than a pulled tooth.'

'Look, Alex,' the colonel began, but Alex cut him off.

'There's something you're not telling us,' Alex said. 'In fact, you admitted as much when you somehow persuaded me to get involved. And I did, as a favour, because I would be helping an old friend, helping you, and that in the end this would all be passed on to someone other than me. Now though, I'm pretty sure that's not how this is going to play out, is it?'

Rachel said, 'What have you gotten us into, Colonel?

Because I'm telling you right now, I didn't ask for it and I'm not happy and I need answers. We need answers.'

The room stood silent and expectant.

Alex was about to speak, to demand some kind of response, when the colonel leaned forward to rest his arms on his knees, his hands clasped in front of his face. His irritation at their arrival was now gone, replaced, Alex thought, by a sense of confused fear written into the older man's face, as though a memory long forgotten and awful had just that moment surfaced.

'Kosovo,' the colonel said.

Alex turned a confused look to Rachel who shrugged.

'What's a war that ended twenty years ago got to do with this, with us?' Alex asked.

The colonel fell silent again and reached a hand down to his dog. Reggie, still on his back, flopped over then shuffled over to nuzzle the hand of his master.

'Sir ...' Alex said.

'It's a long time ago, but seems like last week, to be honest,' the colonel said, keeping his eyes low, his hand stroking his dog. 'I'd seen combat before, but Kosovo was something else.'

'I thought it was a peace-keeping force,' Rachel said.

The colonel raised his eyes and a dark smile cut across his mouth. 'I think we all know that phrase is little more than sugar coating for the pill of war to make it easier for the public to swallow.'

'What happened?' Alex asked.

'We were on the outskirts of Kosovo and had to clear through some buildings,' the colonel said. 'It was pissing down, had been all day, and we were all soaked and freezing and just wanted to get back to some hot food and shelter.'

'Been there often enough,' Alex said, forcing himself to

ignore his own memories and to listen to what the colonel was clearly finding it difficult to tell them.

'There was one last building to check through. It looked as smashed up as the rest except that it had clearly had some rushed repair work done to it. You know, stuff pulled from other buildings to keep it almost standing, blocked-up holes, sheets of plastic covering windows.'

'So you went in?'

'Did a quick recce, but it was quiet and the rain was getting worse, kicked up by a wind that had ice in its breath, and we knew that we'd at least be dry inside.'

The colonel leant back into his chair. 'It was a brothel,' he said. 'Or had been, anyway. We checked out the ground floor, beds in all the rooms, Christ alive it was filthy. And the smell of the place; you could taste it in the back of your throat. Then we went upstairs ...' The colonel's voice broke again and he tried to disguise it with a cough. 'The smell, that was the first thing we noticed. I mean downstairs had been pretty rough but it was like it had been waiting for us at the top of the stairs.'

'What was it?' Rachel asked.

'Death,' the colonel answered, 'but not like you or any of us in here would recognise it. We were in a house and a body can certainly fill a place once it starts to rot, right? But this was, I don't know, thicker? Does that make sense? We had to fight our way through it. Two of the lads with me threw up. It got into our clothes, under our nails. You could taste it in the back of your throat and swallow it.'

Alex didn't speak but what the colonel was saying reminded him of what he'd experienced when they'd met Matt.

'So what was causing it?' Rachel asked, then added, 'Not that I want to know, to be honest.'

'The upstairs was a hallway,' said the colonel, 'about a dozen rooms leading off on both sides. The first was sort of empty.'

'Sort of?' Alex said.

'The bed,' the colonel said, rubbing his eyes with his right hand. 'The bed was ... well, there were bits of whoever had last been in it. We could make out chains, a leg, a hand, but the rest of the body was just sort of scattered. I've never seen anything like it. I mean, it looked like it had exploded, but there was no evidence anywhere of explosives, no shrapnel, no damage to any of the room, no burn marks, nothing. It was just the body, or what was left of it.'

'A body can't just explode,' Rachel said. 'It can't. It doesn't happen. They can burst or split, but that's different to exploding.'

Alex caught the colonel's eye and nodded for him to continue.

'From that point onwards it just got worse and worse. It would be impossible to do what had been done there even if you were armed with a chainsaw. The rooms were a masterpiece of death and violence. Upturned furniture, shattered beds, blood, bone and, well, meat. Someone had gone through that place and killed almost everyone there.'

'Almost?' From the way the story was going, Alex hadn't been expecting survivors.

'I was on point,' the colonel said. 'It was my patrol but after what we'd seen in that place I wanted to be the first in. If I didn't have enough about me to do it, there was no way I was going to expect the rest to do the same.'

Leading by example, Alex thought. He wasn't surprised: the colonel had a way about him that made you know he lead not by giving orders alone, but by being in the thick of things with those who served under him. Not every officer would agree it was good practice to always be at the sharp end, but it as something Alex respected enormously, as did any soldier.

'I was walking along the hall towards the final door. It seemed darker for some reason, like the closer I got the less I could see. The door was ajar so I pushed it open with my boot.'

Alex shivered. Had it grown cold suddenly or was it just the colonel's story sending a chill through him? Or both?

'The first thing I saw was a girl. She looked thirteen, was probably younger.'

'And she was alive?'

'Very much so,' the colonel said. 'She was sitting on what looked from where I was standing like a large chair surrounded by lumps and shapes in the darkness that I couldn't make out at all. I thought it was piles of rags and blankets. I tried to get her to speak but she said nothing, just sat there, staring at me.'

'What did you do?' Rachel asked.

'Lowered my weapon, moved closer,' the colonel said. 'Then I saw ... everything ...' A sob stuttered forth from the colonel and he bucked forwards to drop his head into his hands. 'No one knew what I saw! No one! It's impossible! No one saw it!'

'What do you mean?' Alex asked. 'Your patrol ...'

'I was in the room alone,' the colonel said, clearly working hard to keep himself together as he continued to explain. 'The door slammed shut behind me. There was no one else in there except me and that girl and ... and that thing ...'

The colonel raised his head then and stared at Alex, his face strangely calm, and Alex wondered if the weight of keeping whatever it was he was telling them inside for so long was finally shifting.

'The chair the girl was sitting on was covered in blades: dozens of knives had been rammed through it, with all the blades sticking out through where she was sitting, cutting into her all over. Her chest, legs, arms, her back. Everywhere you looked, the tips of the knives were sticking out and she was slick with blood, covered in it. Like in that movie, *Carrie*, where that kid gets covered in pig's blood? She should've bled out but she was alive and looking at me. And those shapes around her? I could make out uniforms, but the bodies were unrecognisable, as though something had just picked them up and crushed them into any shape you could imagine.'

'You said something else was there,' Alex said, now wanting the story to hurry to a close because the picture the colonel was painting was already going to stay with him for too long.

'Yes, there was,' the colonel said, nodding. 'It was behind the girl. It looked human but it also didn't. I know, that makes no sense, but that's all I can say. It was this thing, standing there, its body slick and wet with blood, and it was stroking the girl's hair with its hand. And then it spoke my name.'

Alex felt a buzz in his pocket. It was his phone, but whoever it was, they'd have to wait. 'What did it say?'

'Just that,' the colonel said. 'My name. Again and again and again. Kept repeating it over and over. My patrol was trying to break through the door but it wouldn't give. I backed away. The girl just kept on staring and then the thing, whatever it was, it jumped up and just crouched on the back of the chair!'

'Did it attack you?' Rachel asked. 'What happened?'

Colonel Blake was silent, staring into the middle distance. 'I blacked out,' he said. 'Went down like a sack of shit. Talk about embarrassing. What soldier, what officer, does that? But the stench of the place, the heat, must've got to me. When I came round, the thing was on top of me, sitting on my chest.'

'This doesn't make sense,' Rachel said. 'What you're saying, Colonel, well, it sounds like ...'

'Sounds like what, corporal?'

'Like you were seeing things, delusional! You can't have seen any of that, and you know it.'

Colonel Blake leaned in close to Rachel. 'It was on top of me,' he said. 'The weight of it was crushing me. I couldn't breathe. Whatever it was, it was grinning, laughing. Behind it, the girl was screaming. Then, and this is the really fun bit so listen well, it stuck its fingers into my mouth, pulled it open, and vomited Christ knows what down my throat.'

Rachel made to stand, but Alex shook his head and she stopped halfway, dropping back down into the chair.

Alex said, 'What did you do?'

'I slotted the fucking thing, that's what happened!' the colonel said, snatching his eyes from Alex to the corporal. 'I managed to kick hard enough to dislodge whatever that fucking thing was and emptied a full magazine into it, switched mags, emptied another. I kicked it off me, booted it across the floor, and just kept on firing, tore the thing apart, took its fucking head off!'

There was a wildness about the colonel now, Alex realised, and he just lay back and let the man get it all out.

'Have you ever seen what that many rounds can do to a body? Have you? Bits go everywhere. You're painting with blood and flesh and bone. You can hear the stuff as it lands, it gets on you, stings your own skin, bone splinters stab you.

But you know what? When I went for my last mag, it was gone. There was nothing there! Just the girl, screaming, and I did our best to save the girl, kept screaming for the rest of the lads to come and help, but they didn't come, and she'd lost so much blood, and when I tried to move her from the chair, from the blades, it was impossible. She died with her eyes on me, Alex! She stared right into me like she was trying to take some of my life with her, or at least hold onto it for as long as she could!'

'And no one saw this other figure?' Alex asked.

The colonel shook his head. 'I was alone, Alex. No one was in that room. I'd blacked out, woken to whatever that thing was on me, and then ripped it apart with over three hundred rounds!'

'But what about the rest of your patrol? You called for them! Why didn't they come and help? Where were they?'

At this question, Alex was sure that the colonel fell even paler. 'Sir?'

'They ...' The colonel closed his eyes, his hands clasped white-knuckle tight in his lap.

Alex said, 'You said you were in that room alone with the girl and what you saw, whatever it was. What happened to the rest of the patrol? Why didn't they come when you called?'

'Because they were already dead, Alex,' the colonel said. 'Every single one of them.'

'What? How?'

'I don't know,' the colonel said, pain drawing lines into his face. 'When that thing was gone, the girl dead, I realised that the door to the room was open. I scrambled to my feet to get away from what had just happened, from the girl, only to find that ...' The colonel let out a sob, choked it down, spoke again. 'You've seen what an IED can do, right?

I'm not talking about the small ones designed to take a foot, but the bigger ones, designed to take out a patrol, a vehicle? That's what it looked like on the other side of that door. I don't know how it happened, or why, just that while I was passed out, it did.'

'What?' Rachel said. 'They were hit with an RPG or something?'

'No evidence of anything like that,' the colonel said. 'Just ... meat ... It was almost medieval what had happened to them. Not one body was in one piece. Arms were gone, legs stripped to the bone, head torn off and split. I had to wade through them to get out. Can you imagine what that's like? I was covered in them when I finally got out. I've never seen anything like it, until now, until this.'

The colonel breathed slow and deep.

'They never found the girl. Just that godawful chair, the blood ...'

'But how can that and all of this be connected?' Rachel asked. 'Whatever it was, it's years ago. I don't get it.'

'I mean, where could she have gone?' the colonel said. 'She was dead! She couldn't be anything else! So where the fuck did she go?'

The colonel let out a long sigh, the weight of what he'd shared gone from him.

'Whoever sent me the feed from the helmet cams of Matt's team knows what happened in that room,' the colonel said. 'Even though it was only me in there and even though I've told no one about it until now, they know and they somehow have access or links to the military because how else could they send me what they did? And that means that what happened to me, and what's happening now, are linked. I just don't know how or why.'

Alex's pocket buzzed again and he pulled out his phone

and answered it on speaker so the colonel and Rachel could hear. The voice at the other end of the call was a muffled sob. 'Becky? What's wrong? What's happened?'

'It's Matt,' Becky said, her voice a broken whisper. 'He's just called, Alex! He's on his way here!'

CHAPTER TWENTY-ONE

Alex's breath caught in his throat.

'Are you absolutely sure, Becky? You're sure that's what Matt said?'

Rachel shook her head and mouthed, 'It can't be.'

'I know,' Alex mouthed back.

It was at least two hours from Hereford to where they'd seen Matt and that time had only been achievable because of Rachel's car and devil-may-care attitude to driving. Alex knew that there was no way Matt could've made the same distance on foot. And there had been no transport at the site of the hospital either, or none that he could recall seeing.

A scream hacked its way out of Alex's phone.

'Becky? Becky!'

More screaming, the sound of a scuffle, then silence.

'The hell is going on?' Blake asked.

For a moment, the phone was silent.

'He's here! Oh shit, he's here, Alex! Matt's here!'

'He can't be,' Rachel said. 'That's impossible!'

Alex nodded to the colonel and Rachel and said, 'Becky, you need to listen to me, okay?'

The response was little more than a muted sob.

'I'm going to call someone right now, okay?' Alex went to say something else but the colonel snatched the phone from him. 'Sir, what the hell?'

The colonel shook his head. 'No one else is getting involved in this,' he said, raised the phone to his mouth and said, 'Becky? This is Colonel Blake. We're on our way. We're coming. But you need to get somewhere safe. Can you do that?'

'Who are you? I don't know who you are! Put Alex back on! Please!'

Colonel held the phone out for Alex. 'No one else,' he said. 'Do you understand?'

Alex didn't understand at all and with his eyes drilling hard into the colonel he took the phone and spoke. 'Becky?'

'He's coming up the stairs, Alex!' Becky's voice was barely a whisper.

'Where are you, Becky? Are you safe? The kids?'

'We're in the airing cupboard,' Becky said. 'Top of the stairs. He's smashing the place up, Alex! Please, hurry!'

Alex was moving fast, Rachel in front, the colonel behind. Rachel kicked her car into life as Blake jumped in behind, Alex taking the passenger seat and heaving the door shut as they took off.

'Know where we're going?' Alex asked.

Rachel nodded, her eyes on the road ahead as she skilfully threaded it down the street ahead.

'Becky, just stay quiet,' Alex said, working hard to sound calm, to keep Becky with him. 'He won't hurt you, Becky, okay? He won't hurt his family, his kids.'

A gasp cut down the line.

Colonel Blake dipped his head between the front seats. 'Come on, Corporal! Move it!'

'You do know it's hours away, right?' Rachel said.

The colonel just stared back and Rachel dropped a gear, took a roundabout sideways on, and sent the colonel tumbling across the back seat. He had no time to recover as she accelerated out of the slide with ease.

For the next few minutes, as Rachel continued on her quest to break all of the speed limits in as short a time as possible, Alex's phone was quiet and he could only hope that that was a good sign, that Becky and the kids were okay, and that Matt had decided to leave them alone. He was relieved when he heard again the voice of his old friend's wife. 'Alex? He's gone. He's left.'

Alex sighed with relief. If Matt had indeed left then at least that might give them the window of time they needed to get there before he came back again. 'You're sure, Becky? Absolutely sure?'

'Yes,' Becky said. 'He's gone. Out the front door I think. Can't hear him anywhere in the house.'

Alex thought for a moment. They had a difficult choice now: Becky could make a break for it, leave the house, go for help, and hope she was right about Matt. If she wasn't, that was only going to end up bad, Alex thought. The alternative was to sit tight until they arrived. It wouldn't be comfortable and it wouldn't go any way to making the two kids feel any better, but at least this way Matt still didn't know where they were.

With a deep breath to calm himself, and to ensure he sounded calm when talking to Becky, he explained to her what he wanted her, Henry and Scarlett to do.

'I'm not sure, Alex,' Becky said, once Alex had finished his explanation. 'What if the kids need the loo or something?'

'You'll just have to make do,' Alex said. 'Tough, I know,

but this is the safest way, okay? We're a couple of hours away now. I'll send you a text when we're nearly there. Have you enough stuff to keep warm?'

Becky said, 'Spare duvets, one of Matt's old sleeping bags, some pillows, towels, yeah, I think we'll be good.'

'Excellent,' Alex said. 'Now try and get some sleep and we'll be there as soon as we can.' And with that, he hung up.

'That was well done,' the colonel said. 'We'll be there soon enough, yes, Corporal?'

As if in answer to that, Rachel accelerated, pushing Alex and the colonel back in their seats.

'Once this is all over, we're going to have a little chat,' Alex said, his eyes on the colonel.

'You make that sound like a threat,' the colonel said.

'It is,' Alex said.

A PUNCH on the leg woke Alex and he stirred from his slumber, whatever pictures and images from his dreams still left in his mind caught up and spun by his conscious brain to drift off as leaves from a tree.

'What?'

'We're nearly there,' Rachel said. 'Five minutes max.'

Alex grabbed his phone and sent a text to Becky: 'There in five. Hold tight.'

The reply came immediately with a thumbs-up emoji.

Ahead, the road was winding and dark, but Hereford's glow was only a spit away Alex saw.

'Two minutes,' Rachel said.

Alex's phone buzzed. He raised it up close to his face, his voice barely audible. 'Becky? Everything okay? We're a minute away, that's all.'

A scream answered him, jostled between the sounds of

children crying, wood being pulled apart, and an animalistic roar which sent a flood of fear-induced adrenaline through Alex's body. 'Becky? Becky! We're almost there! Hold on!'

More screaming down the phone, the roar growing louder, the children's cries turned now to screams.

'Alex! He's here! He's come back! Alex! Help! Alex!'

Rachel swung her car into a hard left, catching the tail as it span out, accelerated, and a few seconds later brought them to a dead stop outside Becky and Matt's home.

Leaping from the car, Alex caught sight of curtains twitching, neighbours wondering just what the hell was going on. What he didn't need right now was people getting involved, trying to help, because he didn't know what he was going to find, and he didn't want people getting hurt. Trouble was, this was army housing and the folk that lived here, though they didn't go looking for a fight, they were quick to get into one if the opportunity arose.

Alex raced up the path to the front door, which had been seemingly kicked from off its hinges. 'We're here, Becky!' Alex yelled into his phone. 'We're here!'

No answer came, but that didn't matter now. They were at the house and Alex stepped across the front step, Rachel and Colonel Blake fast on his heels. He tried the lights, but there was nothing. He wished he was armed, but this wasn't a military operation and they were on home turf. He'd just have to roll with it and improvise if necessary.

'Becky? Becky!'

An eerie silence settled around Alex as he stepped into the house and for a moment he could have believed that all evidence of the outside world beyond the door had been sucked away. The house was draped in darkness, a place of shadows shaped like furniture.

With a hand signal, Alex had Rachel and the colonel

quickly check the lounge and kitchen as he moved towards the stairs. The colonel may have outranked him, but they both knew that in a situation like this, Alex was the one with the recent experience. Both returned with a shake of their heads and Alex placed his left foot on the first step with no idea what he was going to find when he reached the landing.

'Matt? It's Alex. I just want to talk, okay?' Alex's voice rang out like a bell in a cold church, but there was no echo, and it was as though his words were sucked from existence as soon as they were said, replaced by a silence which was growing thicker as he climbed up into the house, crowding him in. Two steps later Alex's ears popped and the staircase in front of him swam a little, forcing him to grab the banister.

Rachel put a hand out to steady him. 'You okay?'

Alex nodded a yes and continued on his way up. But he wasn't okay at all. Something was wrong here, very wrong. He sensed it, deep down, and that was a place he didn't really like venturing anymore.

As he slowly drew closer to the final step, his eyes trying to work out the shapes in the darkness ahead, he was given to the sensation that where they were now had the feel to it of a vast, cold, vaulted room, a cathedral reaching up and out beyond them. It made no sense, he knew that, and yet it was still how it all felt, as though were he to shout out again, his voice would race off into an echo. But even though that was how it seemed on the surface, Alex sensed something else, something brooding in the darkness, watching and waiting, as though this space was both here in the now and somewhere else, and that a door to another place had been opened within it, and from that door something was seeping out, no ... reaching and seeking him out, like the tentacles of some vast and impossible creature hunting its prey. And that reminded him of something, from a long time ago, but that had nothing to do with this. Couldn't. Impossible. And yet he could do nothing to ignore the memories, frayed at the edges though they were, of being dragged into darkness, facing off against an evil of such insanity and impossibility it had led him to the church.

A buzz from his pocket brought Alex back into the present and he pulled out his phone as he took a final step up and onto the landing. In front of him in the dark was what was left of the airing cupboard, the door in pieces, ripped apart like cardboard, clothes and towels and sheets scattered, the space empty.

Alex answered the phone. 'Becky?'

From the speaker came a faint hiss, the sound of breathing.

Alex spoke again, moving away from the airing cupboard and towards the main bedroom. 'Becky? Where are you? We're here, but the house is empty. Where's Matt?'

The voice that replied was neither Becky's nor Matt's, but both, twisted and knotted together and rasped with a pained, agonised and excited joy. 'We're here,' it said. 'Waiting.'

CHAPTER TWENTY-TWO

No sooner had the voice spoken than the house burst into light, every bulb in every room sparking into life, blinding Alex, Rachel and the colonel, and washing the walls with a whiteness which, against the dark it had sent scurrying, seemed even more stark and piercing.

'Bloody hell!' the colonel said, shielding his eyes from the brightness.

Rachel said, 'So, where are they? They have to be here, right? They can't have just disappeared. You were only just speaking to Becky when we arrived!'

Alex knelt down for a closer look at the now smashed airing cupboard. The door hadn't just been yanked open, it had been torn to pieces, bits of it lying all over the place, as though a wild animal had been at it, shredding it with its claws. The space behind it, where Becky had told him she was hiding with Henry and Scarlett, was empty, but on closer inspection, Alex found a small toy car and a little teddy bear, evidence enough that Becky and the kids had indeed been there as they'd raced up the path to the house to find them. So where the hell were they now?

A shout from the colonel from somewhere else in the house pulled Alex from out of the airing cupboard. 'What is it?'

'You need to see this,' the colonel replied.

Alex made his way to where the colonel had called him from and found the man standing in the main bedroom, Rachel close behind. Stepping through the door, Alex was drawn again to the sense that somehow, something was reaching out for them – for him – the inky tentacles he'd earlier sensed in the darkness, half wondered if he'd imagined, still here, somehow slipping through the space between spaces. Not that that made any sense at all, Alex thought, and shook his head as much to dislodge it of the nonsense tying his mind up in knots, as to keep him alert.

The room was, to all intents and purposes, normal. It contained a bed, king-sized by the look of it, and no surprise considering the size of Matt, Alex thought. A bedside cupboard stood sentry at the far end of the bed, one each side, and it was easy to see which was Becky's, not just because it was the only side slept in, but because that particular bedside cupboard was piled high with books, hers and ones she obviously read to the kids. A large wardrobe stared silently from against the wall in front of the bed and between it and the window was a vintage dressing table with a mirror. And that, Alex thought, was all he wanted to find; signs of a normal life, a normal family. Except that the normality of these items stood out in almost violent protest against what was staring back at them from the walls and from the ceiling.

'I checked the other rooms,' the colonel said. 'No sign of Becky, no sign of the kids. This is the only one that looks like this ...' The man sighed heavily as he gestured around the room with his hands.

'What in God's name is this, Padre?'

Alex couldn't answer. All he could do was stare.

The room had been, for want of a better word, Alex thought, decorated, and he had to assume it had been done by Matt. The walls, the ceiling, the mirror on the dressing table, were every inch covered in the same symbols and words they'd found behind the wardrobe and at the hospital, but now the room was covered, the lettering fresh and dark and merging into each other, dripping onto the floor, across the bed. Not an inch had been spared. Even the furniture and the floor stared back through red wet scrawl.

Alex moved over to a wall for a closer look, reaching out a finger to dip into the substance that had been used. He knew what it was, not just in his gut, but because of the iron-like smell in the air.

'It's blood, isn't it?' Rachel said, as Alex rubbed the stuff between finger and thumb, and sniffed it.

'Yes,' he said. 'It's blood.'

Whose it was, he wasn't about to guess at, because right now he needed to believe that Becky and the kids were alive, and that whatever was going on with Matt, whatever they'd already all witnessed and spoken about, required them to be alive. But on top of that, Alex was having problems working out how, if it had been Matt, he'd had time to do it in the first place. It just didn't add up to the chain of events that had happened over the past few hours.

Ignoring the colonel and Rachel, Alex took out his phone and started to take photos of what was in front of them. Then he switched to video and filmed it.

'It's gibberish,' the colonel said. 'Matt ... he's gone mad.'

It was while he was filming that Alex spotted it, something he hadn't noticed when he'd first stepped into the room: a symbol, like a star with seven points, trapped inside a circle. And by the time he'd finished filming and stuffed his phone back in his pocket, he knew the colonel was wrong. 'It's not gibberish,' he said. 'I've seen this before, or something like it, back when ...' And it was the *back when* which was really bothering him now, which was why his voice broke on the words, because his conversion hadn't been because he'd met God. No. If he was truly honest, it was because he'd met the opposite of whatever God was or was supposed to be. And that symbol had not just been a part of it, but right at its very centre.

A sound from downstairs interrupted what Alex was saying.

Alex was out of the room and at the top of the stairs in a beat. He didn't want anyone coming upstairs to see what they were now staring at. He had to stall.

As Alex rounded the top of the stairs, what he expected to find was a concerned neighbour, someone coming over to investigate what was going on, see if they could help. But what stared up at him from the hallway were two small children, the grime and blood on their faces streaked by their tears. 'Henry? Scarlett?'

Alex half ran half fell down the stairs, sweeping up the two children in his arms as though they were his own. He squeezed them tight, as tight as he would had they been his own, and as he held them, waiting for the tears, for something, they remained still. And that worried him even more. 'It's okay,' Alex said, his voice soft and calm. 'We're here now. You're safe.'

There was still nothing from either child and Alex released them, sitting back a little to look at them. Their faces were calm, he noticed, emotionless.

'They took Mummy,' Scarlett said. 'They took her. They've gone.'

Alex said, 'Who took your mummy, Scarlett? Do you know where she is? What about your daddy?'

No answer came, neither did any tears.

Alex, guessing they were both in shock, knew he had to reassure them that they were safe if he was going to get an answer to what had happened to them.

'You're safe,' he said. 'We just need to find your mummy. Did your daddy take her? Did he tell you where they were going?'

At this, Henry spoke and, like Scarlett, his voice was eerily calm.

'We don't know,' Henry said. 'We want to stay with the kind lady.'

'Your dad's not well,' Alex said, not wishing to make things even more confusing because it was clear to him just by the way they were behaving that this was all too much for two small children to take in. 'He just needs us to help him, okay?'

Alex sensed a presence behind him and looked up to find Rachel and the colonel staring down at him.

'I'm assuming I'm not the kind lady,' the colonel said.

Rachel said nothing, just crouched down beside Alex. Without a word, Henry and Scarlett turned from Alex and moved over to Rachel, who took them in her arms.

Alex said, 'All they've said is that Becky was taken. I've asked if it was Matt, and I can't think why it would be anyone else, but they're not saying any more, but ...'

'But what?' the colonel said.

Alex relayed what Scarlett had said, that they had taken Becky. If it was a they, he thought, then who was with Matt? He almost didn't want to know the answer. Because if Matt had brought with him the still squirming and impossible visions of hell from where he'd been imprisoned, then just where was all this leading?

Rachel said, 'Why are they so quiet?'

'Just scared, I think,' Alex said, seeing the concern in Rachel's eyes. 'Can't blame them, really.'

Rachel led Henry and Scarlett through to the living-room then nipped through to the kitchen to make them a glass of squash each, grab some biscuits from a cupboard, and had them sitting quietly in front of the television. Colonel Blake and Alex stood together by the lounge door and Rachel joined them. 'What are we going to do now?' Rachel asked.

Alex stared at Henry and Scarlett for a moment then walked out into the hallway and back into the kitchen, wondering just how to answer. He had no idea what to do next because he had no idea what they were dealing with or why. The footage from the helmet cams, well that could be explained away, he was sure of it. He'd been in similar situations himself, flushing out a cave system, low on ammunition, down to fists and blades. At that point nothing makes sense because you're probably going to die and the memories of those experiences never leave you. And sometimes, all it takes is a trigger, just one more extreme experience, and the foundations of your sanity turn to quicksand. Counselling could only do so much, and sometimes the stress was more than the human mind could manage. Was that what had happened to Matt? If it was, it still didn't explain what had happened at the facility where they'd visited him. Or the writing they'd found upstairs in the bedroom and at the hospital. Nothing did. It was wrong and impossible and a nightmare and ... and nothing, Alex realised. What he'd seen was what he'd seen. Rachel had been there and experienced it. They were no longer dealing with one of his old pals from the Regiment whose head had tripped a switch sending him into a dangerous case of PTSD. This was something much, much worse. Just how much worse he didn't want to consider because what every part of his soul was telling him simply couldn't be true. His own faith had taught him that good was real and so was evil. He believed in an after-life, or at least he sort of did. There had to be something after all this, but the concepts of Heaven and Hell he'd always viewed as exactly that: concepts. What they were in reality he had never been sure of. Was Heaven a place of rolling hills and babbling brooks and happiness and your family and friends and joy and light? Was it a physical thing, a bodily experience, but in a new, heavenly body? Was it a spiritual domain? As to Hell, well that was even more baffling. Why would a supposed all-loving God either create or allow such a place to exist? How could eternal torment be a thing? Was it just distance from God? Was it wailing and gnashing of teeth? These were questions that often roamed around his mind, but now, with what had happened since the colonel had burst in on that fight, they were front and centre. It was making his brain hurt.

'You okay?'

Alex sensed his arm being gently shaken and looked down to see Rachel's hand gripping his elbow. 'Yes, sorry, I was just thinking,' Alex said.

'And?'

Alex pulled his phone out and flicked through the photos he'd taken of the bedroom and of Matt's hospital room. Something was bothering him, something about what they'd seen ... the writing and the symbols ... and then there he was, flicking through old memories of the days he'd been in training, not to be a soldier, but one of God's representatives among them.

'I need to get home,' Alex said, moving to the front door and opening it. 'I've still got all my notes and books from when I was doing my training. I'm sure I've seen something like this before.'

'I'm guessing you don't mean what you got up to during Selection and after, right?'

Alex said, 'The only spiritual side of anything to do with the SAS was heading to the bar after an OP.'

'You'll have to do some driving then,' Rachel said. 'Otherwise I'm going to fall asleep at the wheel.'

'That won't be a problem,' Alex said. 'We won't be taking your car.'

Rachel went to speak but Alex didn't give her a chance and instead just pointed outside. 'Someone's nicked your wheels.'

CHAPTER TWENTY-THREE

'You fucking what?' Rachel raced outside, but there was nothing she could do. The car was on bricks, the wheels all gone.

'This is supposed to be the safest place in the country!' Rachel said, clearly working hard to not lose it completely. 'SAS town! Special Forces ground zero! And some bastard's had the balls to nab my wheels? I'll kill them!'

The colonel was at Alex's side when Rachel returned to the house still fuming.

'What was that you were saying?' the colonel said.

Alex had his phone out and was flicking through his contacts.

'About your notes, something about your training? SAS?'

Alex pulled up a number, tapped it. 'No,' Alex said. 'After that. Church stuff.'

Rachel was still ranting and raving, wishing all kinds of hell and horror onto the 'absolute bastards' who had 'just signed their fucking death warrant,' and it gave Alex a moment of light relief while he waited for an answer. When it came, the conversation was brief and he killed the call barely a minute later.

'Who was that?'

Alex gestured at the houses around them. 'I'm home,' he said to the colonel. 'Means I can call in a favour, right?'

'Wheels?'

Alex gave a sharp nod as a rumble from above made the darkness of the night seem to sink closer.

'Yeah, why not?' said Rachel, now ranting at the sky as a few raindrops started to fall. 'Because rain is exactly what we need!'

'Transport is sorted,' Alex said.

'What about my wheels?'

'Call your insurance,' the colonel suggested.

The rain was coming on strong now and the three of them moved back inside.

'I'll stay with the kids,' the colonel said. 'Someone has to. And I'm guessing that if I even suggest the corporal here is the one to do it she'll have me in a full nelson accusing me of sexism before ripping my head off.'

Rachel was calm enough to say, 'Yeah, pretty much.'

'Sure you'll be okay?' Alex asked. 'And you're still sure you don't want to get anyone else involved?'

'Even if I wanted to, what would I say?' the colonel said. 'We've a lunatic on the loose who's brought the dead back to life and nabbed his wife?'

Rachel said, 'You'd think we would be hearing something by now about the hospital, though, right? I mean, there's no way an event like that can be shut down and hushed.'

'Yes there is,' the colonel said. 'A "D" notice will be in place already, which means if any newspaper does hear about it, they are unable to report it.'

'What happens if they do?'

'You don't want to know.'

Alex dipped his head into the lounge. Henry and Scarlett were still in front of the television, both of them sitting perfectly still. Whatever they had been watching had finished and the screen was now just blank.

'I've never seen anyone react to a traumatic event quite like this before, but then they're kids, so perhaps it's different.'

The colonel pushed past and sat down on the sofa. 'May as well get comfortable.'

Outside the sound of an engine rumbled in through the rain.

Alex said, 'I'm not good with comfortable, so if it's all the same with you, Sir, we'll head back to my place, see if I can find my old notes. It's a long shot but it might help us get to the bottom of all this.'

FIFTEEN MINUTES later and Alex was behind the wheel of a Land Rover Wolf, a vehicle based on the Land Rover Defender. Considerably upgraded from the base model, the extra investment had never gone into making them more comfortable to drive. Which was why, on jumping in, Alex had wound down the window to allow himself some elbow room at the very least. This was the longer wheelbase version, the 110, as the shorter version, the 90, was being sold off by the MOD. It was raining now and Alex was pleased that at least it wasn't like the last version he'd driven, the WMIK, or Weapons Mount Installation Kit. He'd been on another job that the public would never know anything about, racing the thing across some arid, rock-strewn wasteland, carrying out reconnaissance, when his four-man, two-vehicle squad, had been pinged by a large group of enemy combatants tooled up and looking for a rumble. They'd got one, too, he recalled with a grim smile, flexing his left fist as he remembered the vibrations from the belt-fed grenade launcher he'd used to hammer them into oblivion.

'So that's how the SAS works, is it?' Rachel asked, trying to adjust the notoriously loud and ineffective heater. 'You just rock up, knock at the door, and somehow you all know each other, and here you go, mate, have a Landy?'

'Basically, yes,' Alex said. 'Depends though.'

'On what?'

'On whether you've kept your gob shut or not.'

'How do you mean?'

'The Regiment doesn't take too kindly to kiss and tell,' Alex said. 'One thing you learn is that no one talks. No one. About anything. Regiment business stays as exactly that. It doesn't get talked about on the radio, on TV, in books.'

'Bollocks,' Rachel said through a laugh. 'You lot can't stop writing books, doing documentaries, appearing on reality TV.'

'Anything you actually see or hear is sanctioned,' Alex said. 'Trust me: there's not a damned thing in any book or apparent expose, any test on any of those stupid shows for fitness freaks who think they're tough enough, that tells you anything at all. Smoke and mirrors, that's all it is. Make the public think they've been given a secret so that their attention is diverted elsewhere.'

'I'm not convinced,' Rachel said. 'Business is business, right? If the money's good enough ...'

'You don't join the Regiment to make money,' Alex said.

Rachel was silent for a moment, then said, 'So if it wasn't the promise of fame and fortune and your face in silhouette for interviews for the rest of your life that made you join the SAS, what was it? And what about this whole padre thing? You're almost as fucked up as all of this, Alex. And that's saying something.'

Alex eased off the accelerator and started to indicate left. They were nearing home at long last and even though he knew what he needed was sleep, he'd be up in the loft as soon as they got back; his notes were somewhere up there and he'd never be able to sleep anyway until he had some kind of answer to what was happening.

Visiting the Regiment had made sense, not least because Alex couldn't think of any other option open to them. He'd sent a message to an old friend in Hereford, told them enough but not too much, and they had not only sorted them with wheels but were going to send a few lads around to Matt's place to keep eyes-on and make sure everything was, in officer speak, tickety-boo. And, if Matt did come back, they were exactly who you would want waiting to greet him.

Alex finally answered Rachel's question, saying, 'I just wanted to see if I could do it. Turned out, I could. Simple as that.'

The conversation died as the motorway lights gave way to darker roads and country lanes until, at long last, they arrived back at Alex's home. He nudged Rachel awake as he pulled the vehicle to a stop.

'Come on,' Alex said. 'Hot chocolate and biscuits I think, don't you?'

Inside his house, Alex settled Rachel down in the lounge and headed off upstairs. The loft was a cosy cave system of boxes and holdalls and Bergens. It wasn't that Alex was a hoarder as such, just that he wasn't a big fan of throwing something away which could one day prove to be useful. Which was something completely different, or at least that's what he'd always told himself.

It took a few minutes to clamber through to where his theology stuff was located and on the way Alex bumped into a few more memories than he would've liked. But perhaps that was half the reason he kept all this stuff, he thought, lifting the box of files and papers and books back over to the ladder leading out of the attic. If he got rid of everything, he'd be losing a part of himself; the memories, the experiences, they were all a part of what he now was, and it helped him to make sense of the strange path he'd decided to take.

Alex walked into the lounge and dropped the box in front of his favourite chair. Rachel was asleep but quickly stirred awake. She checked her phone. 'Nothing from the colonel,' she said.

'No news is probably good news,' Alex said.

Rachel leaned over the box and pulled out a handful of books to read the spines. 'Weird ...'

Alex was searching through some old lecture notes. 'What is?'

'I just thought it would all be Bible stuff,' Rachel said. 'But this one's about witchcraft and this one's about sexuality.'

'I like to read around my subject,' Alex said, unwilling to offer the truth of it, talk about what had happened on the streets of Bristol all those years ago, because it was then that he'd last seen a certain symbol, one he was now trying to find his notes about. 'It's like we say in the SAS, right? Train hard, fight easy? Same rule applies: study hard, learn easy. Or something.'

Alex moved on to another pile of notes and had soon exhausted everything in the box. Remembering then that there were more somewhere in the darkness above, he was in the loft again and back downstairs a few minutes later with two more boxes and a beaten up leather satchel.

Rachel reached for the satchel. 'Now this I like,' she said, opening it and removing from inside a leather-bound book which had clearly seen better days. 'And this is exactly what I expected to find. Does it come with a little bottle of holy water?'

Alex looked up to see Rachel holding his old Bible in one hand and a small wooden cross in the other. 'How do you mean?'

'It's like an exorcist's, well, exorcism kit, isn't it?' Rachel said. 'You trained in all that as well?'

Alex shook his head.

'I'm Church of England, not Catholic. We're more tea and cake than demons and damnation.'

Rachel placed the items back in the satchel. Alex kept on digging.

'So Catholics believe in Hell and demons and you lot don't?'

'Not what I said,' said Alex. 'Church of England just isn't quite into it so heavily. I mean, it doesn't have professional exorcists for a start.'

'Professional?'

'You can't just do an exorcism,' Alex said. 'There's all kinds of hoops that have to be jumped through before an exorcism is even considered, and even when it is, they call in a specialist, once they've decided it's for real and not some kind of mental illness or whatever.'

Rachel laughed. 'You mean, they're like Special Forces priests?'

'No,' Alex said. 'And yes. I suppose. I don't know. But

they're trained and yes it does involve a Bible and a crucifix and holy water. Just like in the movies.'

Rachel raised an eyebrow. 'Sounds far-fetched,' she said. 'Coffee?'

Alex said yes, but as Rachel made to leave said, 'I was right!'

Rachel snapped back around.

'Look,' Alex said, lifting up a book, which was open in his hands, to give Rachel a better look. 'Recognise any of it?' The pages were illustrated with signs and symbols and lettering, all annotated by tiny boxes of text.

'I guess so,' Rachel said. 'What is it?'

'Avestan,' Alex said.

'Avest what?'

'It's a dead language,' Alex said. 'This book is all about monotheism.'

Rachel picked up one of the other books from the box and read the title. It had on the cover a circle inside which a number of lines inter-crossed, coming together in a number of points around its inside edge.

'And this one is about an organisation called The Order of Nine Angles,' Rachel said. 'And that means as much to me as what you just said.

'They're a satanic group,' Alex said, 'that's all you need to know about them.'

Rachel noticed the edge to Alex's voice sharpen a little.

'Sounds like you're not telling me everything.'

'I'm telling you enough,' Alex said, taking the book from her. His last run in with The Order was a nightmare which stalked him still, not least because it took him back to what had caused him to leave the SAS and end up wearing a dog collar. If they were involved in whatever this was then Alex could only guess at the horrors just waiting round the corner.

Rachel let silence take over for a moment and waited for Alex to speak again.

Alex took a long, deep breath then said, 'All early religions were polytheistic, meaning they had lots of gods. So, you know, the sun god and the rain god and the god of rocks and the god of the harvest, or whatever. Lots of gods, right?'

'I'm with you,' Rachel said. 'I'm also impressed. You sound like you know what you're talking about.'

'Monotheism, on the other hand,' continued Alex, 'is the belief in a singular god, which is what this book is about. The origins of Judaism, Christianity, Islam. And this text here?' Alex pointed again at the pages, resting his back against the wall behind him. Rachel sat down beside him.

'This is all about Zoroastrianism, which is an ancient religion from Afghanistan. It's still around, but it's not exactly mainstream. It was the first proper monotheistic religion.'

'And that's important why?'

'It's important,' Alex said, 'because Matt's mission was in Afghanistan. And unless he's been studying ancient dead languages and religion for the past few years, then something happened in those caves that lead to whatever's happening now and –'

'And all that stuff we found written on the bedroom walls in blood,' Rachel said, finishing Alex's sentence for him.

Alex rested his phone on the open pages, the screen showing symbols which matched those in the book.

'They're the same,' Rachel said.

Alex took the book then and read from the pages. 'These symbols and markings refer to Angra Mainyu, a

Zoroastrian demon, also described as a destructive spirit and dweller of darkness.' Alex continued to read from the book. 'It is thought that this particular demon was the foundation for what eventually became the biblical Beelzebub, or Satan.'

'Holy shit,' Rachel said.

'Holy shit indeed,' said Alex.

CHAPTER TWENTY-FOUR

'WELL, IT WOULD BE,' RACHEL SAID, 'IF I ACTUALLY believed in any of it.'

Alex was still flicking through his notes, comparing them with the photos on his phone.

'Belief has nothing to do with what happened at the place where Matt was being held,' he said. 'Unless you can think of an entirely rational explanation as to how we were attacked by a man with no head.'

Rachel fell quiet for a moment, then said, 'Whatever it was, what are we going to do about all this? We can hardly call up the Military Police and tell them your ex-SAS pal is possessed by an ancient demon, who may or may not actually be Satan, oh and he's kidnapped his ex-wife, and no we don't know why.'

Alex shrugged, because right then he was more than happy to do just that. 'Look at this,' he said. Alex handed his phone to Rachel.

'What?'

'Tell me what you see.'

Rachel stared at the screen. 'A load of gibberish is what

I see,' she said. 'Apparently it's something called Avestan, but I'll have to take your word for that, won't I?'

'What else?'

Rachel made to protest, but the look on Alex's face told her to have another look. 'Nothing,' she said. 'It's just squiggles and weirdness and numbers.'

'Exactly,' Alex said.

'Exactly what?'

Alex took the phone back. 'Why would Matt paint those numbers? They must mean something. Everything else is, to be frank, stuff he shouldn't have any knowledge of, but the numbers stand out because they're not like everything else, all the other writing and symbols. They're not random.'

'Perhaps he was trying to come up with a lucky number for the lottery,' Rachel said.

'Six numbers,' Alex said, and held his phone between himself and the corporal so that they could both see the screen. 'First we get them here, in the writing behind the wardrobe, right?'

Rachel said, 'Yes, but so what?'

Alex swiped to the next photo. 'Then here, in Matt's hospital room.'

'I don't know what you're expecting me to say.'

Alex swiped to a final photo, this one of the bedroom. 'Then this one. So that's three six-digit numbers.'

Rachel rubbed her temples. 'Help me here,' she said. 'Please.'

'I've a hunch,' Alex said.

'As in that story about Notre Dame,' Rachel said, 'or American cop show?'

'Cop show,' Alex said. 'So, what if the numbers are grid references?'

'That's easy to check,' Rachel said and pulled out her own phone. A moment later, a grid reference finder was live on her screen. 'Give me one of the numbers,' she said.

'It's just a hunch,' Alex said, then read the first set of numbers to her, the ones from behind Becky's wardrobe.

Rachel stared at her phone. 'You're shitting me,' she said then showed the screen to Alex. 'It's the hospital, Alex,' she said. 'The one where Matt was held. No way that's a coincidence.'

'That was the one from behind the wardrobe,' Alex said, then read out the other numbers, first the one from Matt's hospital room, then the final one they'd found in the bedroom after Becky had disappeared. The one from the hospital room was Matt and Becky's house.

Rachel looked at the map on her screen and reduced its size with a pinch of her fingers. 'The third one, from the bedroom, it's Wiltshire,' she said. 'Salisbury Plain.'

'Where exactly? Anywhere specific?'

Rachel looked up from her phone. 'It's Imber,' she said, then added, 'I hate that place. Creeps me out.'

Alex, like anyone who'd done not just basic military training, but any training at all for urban warfare, knew of Imber. 'Last time I was there I was pelted with potatoes. Those things don't half hurt if one catches you in the face. Smashed my nose to a pulp.'

Alex rested his head against the wall he was leaning on. Imber, he thought. Why would the third grid reference – if that's what the numbers actually were – take them there? It was nothing more than an uninhabited village, evacuated in 1943 to help train American soldiers for the D-Day landings. After that it had been used by the MOD for training, particularly soldiers heading off to Northern Ireland during the troubles. New buildings had been added over the years, yet the church and the pub still stood, which was why the place felt a bit strange and eerie, trapped in time almost. And even though a purpose-built urban warfare complex had been built close by to better suit modern training needs for close quarter battle, Imber was still under MOD ownership, still in use, and civilian access restricted.

'So, what now?'

Rachel's question was one Alex was already trying to answer. He had too many questions and they were all joining together to force him to confront things he really only ever dealt with as concepts of belief and faith, not as real, physical things, things that you see and touch. Things that could hurt. He was dealing with enough confusion inside as it was, the soldier and padre fighting for first position, and none of this was helping. Or perhaps it was? All Alex knew right now was that it was all making his head hurt, and no amount of prayer, or illegal bare-knuckle fighting, was going to help.

If he started right at the beginning of it all then he couldn't help but feel suspicious about the mission Matt's team had been sent on. He'd been uneasy about it from the moment the colonel had started to show him what had been captured by those helmet cams, and that was part of the reason he hadn't wanted to get involved, and his unease had only grown. What he'd seen from the footage could on the one hand be seen as nothing more than stress and darkness and violence and hysteria. But it didn't add up, none of it did. From the moment Matt's team had entered the caves, something had been wrong. The carnage was on a scale he'd never seen. The things the soldiers thought or believed they encountered were unbelievable, but soldiers were generally hard to spook, and they certainly didn't make stuff up to the scale witnessed in the footage. Then there was what was found in the cave at the end, the pot, the shackled skeleton of a child, scorched black. INT was never that off, certainly not on a job like that. It didn't make any sense. And from that point forward it seemed to Alex that things had just escalated both in terms of not making sense and also in terms of what they were being confronted with.

To have Matt checked over was sensible and he was sure he would have gone through the now firmly embedded approach to mitigating PTSD among serving personnel. The army had done its best to try to come to terms with its lack of care, or indeed understanding, when it came to what its staff went through and how follow-up care should be provided. But nowhere in any of that did it have secret hospitals. That in itself was so off the scale weird that Alex still couldn't get his head around it. It was almost as if someone knew something about what was happening, or had happened, to Matt, and had decided that the facility was the safest option. Whatever the reasoning, it was very out of the ordinary.

And what about the writing scrawled on the walls, Matt's knowledge of a dead language, an ancient religion? All this from a man who, last time Alex had checked, didn't just not read, but was almost proud of how he didn't waste his time on 'all that made up shit,' as he'd once said, having stared somewhat bemused at the shelves of books Alex had himself always had in his life. So how had Matt gained this knowledge? Who had given it to him? How had he come by it? And for what possible reason?

There were other things, too. The tin of human pineal glands gave him the creeps, more so than what had attacked them after he and Rachel had spoken with Matt. How had Matt come by them, and why? Were they nabbed from a hospital? But why would a hospital store them and how would Matt get them, unless through some hideous, black market dealings? The colonel's own revelation about Kosovo had been an eye opener, and there was a link there, because of the emails, but who – and how? – could or would send them? Was there a link between what the colonel had experienced and all this?

Finally, what about Matt ... This was what Alex was struggling with more than anything. They were old mates, had soldiered together, run missions together, done things which by rights should keep them awake at night for the rest of their lives. They'd seen the best and the worst of humanity and brought it to those who deserved it with astonishing and ferocious violence. But now Matt was something different, almost like he wasn't Matt at all. He had never been the kind of man to bring the war home and take it out on his family. Something had changed in him, something truly terrible. Alex didn't really want to go down this route, but a part of him was thinking that perhaps the Catholic Church had something with its clearer views on possession, because that seemed to be what this was. But it couldn't be, could it? Because possession was little more than fear of the unknown, of mental illness and goodness knows what else. It couldn't be that. But what about what had happened after, when he and Rachel had been attacked? Those images, the footage of it, were still on his phone. It had happened. It was real. Alex had seen a dead man, a corpse ripped apart by a brutal savagery, come at him, grab him, even with its head gone. And if they hadn't got away from there, what would've happened next? And finally, The Order of Nine Angles ... It all seemed so ...

'Alex?'

Alex felt himself shaken and lifted his eyes to see Rachel staring at him. 'Hmm?'

'You drifted off,' Rachel said.

Alex needed answers. 'Yeah, sorry, just thinking about it all.' Alex knew that there really was only one person who could give them to him.

'So, you got a plan?'

And with a hostage involved ... 'Yeah,' Alex said. 'I'm going after Matt.'

CHAPTER TWENTY-FIVE

The church was thick with a darkness which bled from the windows, filling the vaulted space beyond with a suffocating sense of despair. What moonlight there was could barely scratch its way through the thick, grey clouds, which turned and tumbled in the sky above the village of Imber. A silence paraded the dead streets, windows like corpse eyes staring out lifelessly from buildings long ago dead, their own ghosts unable to venture out into the gloom. Most nights, nature's own would walk through the crumbling remains, the furred and feathered keepers of the hours when the rest of the world slept. But this night nothing walked or flew among the brickwork and the air was so still it was as though the world was holding its breath, or choking.

For years now, Betty Webb had attended Imber church. She had been a child when the village had been to all intents and purposes erased from existence. Her heart still broke at the memory of it all and she wondered how more hadn't gone the way of the old blacksmith, who had been found weeping by his anvil, whom everyone believed had died of a broken heart. The war had claimed many lives abroad, in battle, in the skies, but for Betty the war had crept up on her and stolen something precious, a community that was her family and was never allowed to heal. They'd been promised compensation, some had hoped that with the war over, they would be allowed to return home, but they had all been left wanting. And so, when she could, Betty returned, to walk hand in hand with her memories and to talk to ghosts.

What she couldn't quite understand, however, was why she was at the village in the middle of the night, or even remember how she had arrived. It was obvious that she had driven because she had just stepped out of her old and yet very reliable Nissan Micra, its red paint fading, yes, but inside it was as new and fresh as the day she'd bought it fifteen years ago. She just didn't remember the journey. She did remember a little girl, though. Had the girl knocked at her door? Was that it? Yes, perhaps it was. And then Betty had given her a lift to Imber because the girl had said they both needed to go home and that everyone was waiting. Betty knew that was impossible, it just had to be, but sometimes the memories were so strong she was sure that if she put her mind to it she could pull them all around her and live them again. After all, weren't there days when she could still smell her own mother's perfume, her father's pipe tobacco, hear them talking to each other, calling her?

Betty had walked from her car and down into the village. She'd had no idea if she was allowed to or not because she hadn't checked what the date was to make sure she wasn't about to get shot by some soldiers on a training exercise. She'd noticed the quiet of the village, more quiet then she had ever experienced it before, and the way the windows of the buildings seemed to stare at her. Had the girl walked with her? Had she held her hand as they walked? What had they talked about? She couldn't really remember and if they had shared any words those words seemed just beyond reach. Then from the streets she had ambled up to the church, the silence chasing her along, growing behind her at the same time as drawing her on, but to what she didn't know. But she wasn't scared, and that surprised Betty. That was another scar of the war, her fear of the dark, that something would come and take her or kill her in the middle of the night and since then she had only ever been able to sleep with a light on. So walking down an unlit street in a dead village, well that really was something, she thought, and stifled a giggle. After all, wasn't this all rather dangerous and rebellious, even? Particularly as she was in her 80s! How lovely! What her friends would say, she couldn't hazard a guess at, but she didn't care. This was all a lot more exciting than taking another trip to Asda just to be around other people and to brush away the loneliness for a while.

A movement ahead caught Betty's eye. It was the girl! Yes, there she was! Oh, goodness, where had she gone to again? Why did she keep appearing and then disappearing. It was most annoying. So Betty moved forward, deeper into the church. It was cold, but not so cold as to chill her all the way to her bones, as it had when she had sat inside it as a child so long ago. It had been cold then, hadn't it? Icy, even in the height of summer. But she had been kept warm, squashed between her parents, surrounded by family and friends from the village.

'Betty ...'

The voice was small, light, feminine and Betty snapped round to see back towards where she had come into the church, the girl again. What was she doing? Why had she turned up at her house? Why had she brought her here? Something wasn't right, Betty was sure of it, but she couldn't work out what, and the harder she tried to think about it, the further the answer to what it was seemed to drift.

'Betty ...' The girl called her again and Betty walked towards her and it was then that she saw it, a thing she had never seen before, something no one had ever mentioned, and yet there it was, at least part of it, the rest clearly covered over by the whitewash paint which coated the rest of the walls of the church.

Betty stepped nearer for a closer look, stood on one of the pews, and yes she was right, she wasn't imagining it! Here, in front of her, was a painting! How had it never been seen before? It was clearly enormous and very, very old. She could make out faint images of beings – were some of them angels, demons? – and she wondered if it was a 'Doom', those strange and oh so very old paintings painted in churches to depict the Christian view of the Last Judgement. Is that what it was? She had to see more of it. Was this why the girl had brought her here? To discover this wonderful and rather creepy thing? Yes, that was it!

Betty ran to the vestry and was soon back with a cloth and a mug of water. She dabbed the cloth into the water and gave the whitewash covering the painting a little scrub. To her amazement some of it came away, revealing more of the painting! Was that an eye? Yes, it was! A bright, staring eye! How wonderful! Betty scrubbed again, then some more, and was soon in need of more water, so the next time she filled four whole mugs and attacked the white paint as best she could, being an octogenarian and atop a wooden pew in a darkness that, if she had time to notice, now seemed to not be so gloomy, but lit even, though by what, she wasn't sure, but it didn't matter. Oh, what a painting this was! Just look!

It would be a couple of hours before Betty would reveal the whole of the painting. But the little girl was patient. She was used to waiting. They all were. And they had all waited for so long for something like this to happen, a way for them to break down the door which had held them back for eons now, since before anything in Creation had come to have a heartbeat. Since before the time of the stars and the reason for all that now was, setting it all in place with a breath. Other ways had been tried, and those ways had failed, but this? Well, it was too good an opportunity to miss, wasn't it? She'd felt the echo of a possibility of it back when she had first met that soldier, when she had spilled into him her darkness in that building of all those girls she had killed so easily and with such glee, because there was a connection with him in the future that she could make use of, which they would all benefit from, and she had stretched forth herself to find it and touch it and claim it and to also keep it hidden. And now, much to her satisfaction, it was all coming to pass. And when it did, wouldn't it be wonderful? Yes, it would. It would be a glorious and wondrous thing and at last they would be free and could take what was rightfully theirs and if she was to be brutally honest right now she could hardly fucking wait ...

The girl glanced up at Betty who was now revealing the last part of the painting. The Doom itself, the girl knew, had been hidden for centuries, not because it had been kept a secret by the church, but by those like her, the few who managed to break free. It was a key, painted by a man thrown into madness by the visions others like her had given him, images which, when the time came, would be brought to life and open a door.

At first glance, the Doom painting was just that, a painting. But there were differences that would become clear at a closer glance. At its centre, the Christ sat in magisterial judgement over all, his open hands reaching out, the wounds of his crucifixion visible not just here but on his feet and his side. Except it wasn't the Christ at all, but a mockery of God's Son, the crown on his head not of thorns but of bodies writhing in joyous pain, his mouth flicking out a long, blood-red forked tongue, his throne made of bones. At his feet, bowed in worship, were twelve figures, though these were not the disciples of the New Testament, but the four princes of the demons, joined by the eight sub-princes, one of whom the girl had a thing for, Asmodeus, who was indeed a creature that liked to party. Beyond this lay a vast garden, though one which looked scorched and broken. And whereas the ancient vision of judgement was for the dead to rise and be taken to Heaven or thrown into Hell, in this particular vision the dead were all of them doomed, man, woman and child. Creatures pulled them from the earth, forced themselves into their bodies through any orifice they could, the bodies bulging as they were consumed from within, and those already thusly possessed danced in flames, rapture on their faces, dreaming – as the girl did herself and had done for time immeasurable – of what was to come; a freedom so rich, so beautiful, it made her weep.

As Betty stood back to look at her work, the girl, with tears born of the ecstasy of what was to come, reached out her hand, sunk her fingers into the flesh of Betty's ankle, and with a strength that defied the impossible, snapped the old woman down from her perch with a whip crack to slam into the ground so hard that the church echoed for a few seconds to the sound of shattering bones. Then, with Betty still whimpering, long fingers of her steaming blood stretching out along the cold flagstones of the church floor, the girl swept her back up into the air to smash into the painting, the old woman's body bursting with the impact, her skull shattering into a thousand pieces, and blood and brains and gore splattering that which Betty had only moments ago finished revealing.

The silence which followed this ferociously brief assault on an aging and frail human body was disturbed only by a faint slurping, as the painting sucked up the blood with a glee bordering on the delicious.

CHAPTER TWENTY-SIX

The early hours of the new day were not working too well at being welcoming. The heavens were lost behind a black sky of cloud heavy with rain, sheets of it raking across the ground, driven by a wind which seemed intent on knocking Alex and Rachel off their feet as they ran from Alex's house to the Land Rover Wolf. Thunder danced in the darkness, growling and snarling at the world below, as shards of lightning lanced into the earth.

Alex was surprised to find that when they climbed into the vehicle there were no leaks. And that was a first, because he was sure there wasn't a Land Rover on the planet that didn't let the water in.

'You sure this is sensible?' Rachel said, clipping herself into the passenger seat.

Alex did the same behind the steering wheel. 'I don't think sensible is the word I'd use,' said Alex. 'But I also don't think we have much choice, do you?'

Alex slipped the key into the ignition and a moment later the thrum of the diesel engine under the bonnet did its best to sound angry and ready against the thunder crashing around outside.

'And you're sure you don't want to call in some extra support on this? I mean, I've seen Matt and ...' Rachel's voice trailed off.

'I know what you're saying,' Alex said, 'but we can't escalate this because there's no one to escalate it to.'

'You sound very sure.'

'I am,' Alex said. 'You know what we've seen and you know what we found back there in my own house. This isn't just your average case of PTSD gone too far. This is something far, far worse.'

'And you're the man to sort it, right?'

Alex didn't answer that one straightaway because he knew Rachel had a point, that this should be reported upwards and left to someone else to deal with. But, deep down, Alex knew that no one would be able to handle it any better than he, so why involve them? If he was right, if he believed not just his gut but what his own faith told him, and Matt was somehow being controlled by a creature from, well, 'Hell', then wasn't he better placed to handle this anyway? Bullets alone couldn't solve this, neither could a Bible, but perhaps both together had a chance. Not that he was armed, he thought, well, not with anything with a trigger. If there was one thing his time in the Regiment had taught him, it was to improvise.

'I have to,' Alex said. 'Matt is an old friend. Becky needs me.'

'But you said yourself that you're not an exorcist,' Rachel said, 'and I'm stunned I just used that word because this whole thing is crazy.'

Alex turned to glare at Rachel. 'You've seen everything

I've seen,' he said, his voice quiet, steady, menacing. 'Can you explain it?'

Rachel shook her head then said. 'Look, I know there's only one of him, but we're not even armed.'

'Neither is he.'

'You don't know that! And have you forgotten what was coming at us from the doors of the medical facility? What if it's not just Matt we're dealing with! Have you thought about that? What if what we saw came with him? What about that?'

Alex had thought about it but it still hadn't changed his mind as to the course of action they were now taking. He'd thought back to what had happened and wondered how much of what they had seen had been real, how much not. Yes, a dead man had attacked them, but had Matt really been surrounded by more of the same? Or was that some trick of whatever was controlling him? Wasn't the Devil the master of lies? And what if they had actually been hallucinating the whole thing? Was that a possibility? Something from that facility could have got into their system, caused their brain to malfunction under stress. Perhaps. And also, perhaps not, because thinking and overthinking it all was enough to send him over the edge and, right now, Alex had to take action to stop that happening.

'You don't have to come,' Alex said. 'I can do this alone.'

Rachel threw her head back with a laugh both cold and sharp. 'You and your trusty shepherd's crook, right? Who the fuck do you think you are?'

'How do you mean?'

'You're like *Rambo* meets *The Exorcist*, except you don't even have a big, stupid knife, never mind a proper crucifix!'

'That's not funny.'

'It's not supposed to be!' Rachel said. 'That stuff belongs

in the movies, in novels, in stories told around campfires to scare children! This is real, Alex. Your mate, Matt, something is wrong with him, wrong with his head, we've all seen that. And everything else, well, I've no explanation for. But don't go into this thinking you can smash your way through an army of demons or whatever the hell it is, armed with nothing more than your supposed faith, which, from where I'm sitting, isn't exactly unshakable, is it?'

'I know Matt,' Alex said. 'And demons are real, trust me.'

'How can you say demons are real and trust me in the same sentence?'

'What about what the colonel told us?' Alex said. 'You don't think that was a demon?'

'I think it was an old memory twisted by time and nightmares into something more than it was when it happened,' Rachel said. 'Not a demon.'

'I hope you're right,' Alex said.

'You're a padre who does bare-knuckle fighting for stress relief,' Rachel said. 'A padre still haunted by his life in the SAS. Your faith and knowing Matt won't make any difference if you can't keep your head. And talking of demons just makes me think you've already lost it.'

'I can talk him back to us from wherever he's gone ...'

'And what if you can't? You've no answer to that, have you?'

Alex was quiet.

'Have you thought that you might not be able to bring him back? What then? And where exactly are you bringing him back from, Alex?'

'I'll get him back,' Alex said, then pushed the gear lever forward, dropped the clutch, and sent them off into the early hours of the day.

. . .

WHEN THEY ARRIVED, there was still enough of the dark of the night left to give the place the feel of a Hammer House of Horror movie set. The wind had blown the black cloud into scraps of grey, which hung across the sky like torn rags caught in a bush of thorns. The rain had eased, but the air was still damp. The thunder was distant, but it still grumbled, sounding as though it wanted to crawl back across the battered lands below and start all over again. Around the vehicle lay broken bits of branches, torn from the trees and scattered like bones from an upturned coffin. And just ahead in the gloom, its buildings sunk deep in a thick fog rising up from the ground, was Imber.

'Doesn't look all that welcoming, does it?' Rachel said. 'But then again, it never did.'

Alex didn't disagree. The place, the weather, it all reminded him of jobs he'd been on that all too often were a battle between fear and boredom, broken up only by short, sharp bursts of the most intense and exciting violence any human could experience.

Rachel opened her door. 'Any idea where we start?'

Alex said, 'If he's here, we'll find him.'

'You sound very sure about that,' Rachel said. 'Why?'

'He wants us to.'

Outside the Land Rover, the damp in the air clung to Alex and Rachel, beading into droplets on their skin, running down their faces to trace shivers down their backs. Alex had his crook with him, clasped in his left hand. What good it would do he wasn't sure, but it was better than nothing. He saw as well that Rachel was carrying something and, on closer inspection, saw a large wrench in her right hand. She must have found it in the vehicle, he thought.

On they walked, the buildings of Imber silent as sentinels as they walked past. The eeriness of the place only grew the deeper they explored. The darkness behind the windows seemed deeper, thicker than it should be, Alex thought, and if he stared too long into it he was sure that it shifted, but not as though someone was hiding in it. Instead, it was as though the darkness itself was moving, shifting from room to room, building to building, spying on them.

Alex was about to turn right when he felt a tug on his arm and turned to see Rachel pointing down another street. Halfway along it sat a small red car. From this distance he had no idea what it was, but it stood out against the bleak backdrop of a dead village, an out of place symbol of life telling them that someone else was here.

'That's not Matt's car,' Alex said.

'He wouldn't fit in it,' Rachel said, as they drew closer.

'So whose is it? And why are they here?'

Rachel ducked down to look inside the windows, wiping rain from the glass, then stood back up with a shrug.

'Could be just some kids nicked it and dropped it here,' Alex said.

Rachel said, 'No chance. These wheels aren't worth nicking, not even for a joy ride. Anyway, the keys are still in it.'

Alex looked at the buildings around them. If Matt was here, and he was sure he had to be, then he wasn't making it easy to be found.

'Not as though this is a high crime area, is it?' Alex said.

A clatter from behind had Alex turn on his heels, the crook up and behind him rather than in front, ready for a swing if needed.

'See anything?' Rachel said.

Alex shook his head, stared into the gloom. And he

immediately had a sense that the gloom was staring back. Not just from ahead, but from all around them.

'You feel that?' Alex said.

'Yeah,' Rachel said. 'You got eyes on?'

Alex stepped away from the car his senses on fire now, hardwired into the moment. Soldiers developed a sixth sense, something that knew when a threat was approaching, a wiring together of all the senses, each working with the others to make the whole stronger. It had saved Alex's life more times than he could remember.

The gloom shifted. The darkness in the building beside them seemed to pulse. A stench rolled out of nowhere, a mix of rot and char that sunk into the back of Alex's throat and made him gag. Then something stepped into view from around the corner of the nearest building and what Alex saw burned itself into his mind with the heat of the sun.

'Get in the car ...'

'What?'

'I said, get in the car!'

Alex snapped round, ripped open the car door and was behind the wheel with the engine alive before Rachel had even managed to climb in herself.

'The fuck did you see?' Rachel said, struggling with her seatbelt as Alex dropped the gearbox into first and accelerated.

Alex reached up and turned the rear view mirror around so that Rachel could see exactly what he'd seen.

'Jesus Christ ...'

That name was on Alex's lips, too, as he heaved them forward and away from the jaws of Hell.

CHAPTER TWENTY-SEVEN

It was a girl, that was all, Alex thought. A young girl, probably aged no more than thirteen. A young girl in jeans and a T-shirt, bare feet, long brown hair. In almost every possible way there was nothing terrifying about her at all. Nothing out of the ordinary. Nothing that would make you even stop and look twice if you saw her on a normal street on a normal day. Yes, the bare feet would make you wonder if everything was okay, perhaps even cause you to ask if she needed help or had lost her parents, but other than that? Nothing. Not a damned thing. It was what was with her that had them running for their lives, and what she dragged behind her, gripped in her right hand.

'The fuck is that?' Rachel asked, her hands bracing her against the dashboard as Alex swung the vehicle into a hard right.

'The girl or everything else?' Alex asked.

'Every fucking thing else!' Rachel said. 'Every! Fucking! Thing!'

Alex didn't have an answer and knew that there wasn't even any point in trying to find one. The girl, yes, she looked normal, but in almost every way it was that normality which stung so sharply in the vision that had emerged to greet them with her innocent smile.

In the girl's hand was a foot. A pale, white thing splattered in dark blood. The leg attached to it, it's angles were all wrong because a leg shouldn't have angles, just a bend where the knee was, but this limb was so broken, the skin so pierced and torn by the bones ripping out from inside, that it was almost zig-zag. The other leg, or what was left of it, was bent up and behind the body that both it and its fellow belonged to. The body itself was little more than a mess of broken flesh, raw and ripped and ragged and torn, burst organs hanging out, a train of intestines tumbling and twisting with every step the girl was making. Further up, the arms were in much the same state as the legs, but the head was a monstrous salute to an awful death, cracked open like an egg, the face barely more than mince. And yet still that wasn't the worst of it, thought Alex, who was looking to get them out of Imber as quickly as possible, in a car the size of a shopping trolley and just as slow, but was shaking at what they had seen and how quickly the images had imprinted onto his mind.

Behind the girl, behind the awfulness that she dragged with her clasped in her hand, something else was rolling and tumbling and reaching out for them. Alex didn't know what it was because every time he tried to focus his mind on to what he'd seen, the images would change. One moment it was vast prison bars built from a shimmering blackness behind which writhed and jostled and snarled things born of nightmares, twisted visions of humanity ripped from a medieval torturer's scrap book. But then the image would shift, and instead an endless and impossible blasted emptiness would be there, yet for all its emptiness Alex knew that it was reaching out, tendrils of something foul and invisible and hungry dragging it forward. And just when Alex was sure it was going to reach him, that image would be smeared away like ink in a rainstorm and in its place a vision of oceanic horror, a deep and thrumming vessel of darkness twisted into impossible shapes by a light both blinding and searingly hot. And it too reached out, as though trying to pull itself into the now, to escape from wherever held it trapped and riven with rage.

Alex stamped on the brakes. The girl was in front of them now, the vision behind her twisting and turning and boiling like burned caramel in a pan.

'She can't be there!' Rachel said. 'She was behind us! We just left her behind! The hell is going on, Alex?'

Alex wasn't listening. He already had the car in reverse, hooked the steering wheel down with his left hand, dropped back into first gear, screeched off down another street. But something else was bothering him and that was what the colonel had told them about Kosovo, about the girl he'd encountered. And now, here they were, and Alex didn't want to think it, but couldn't help it, because it was just too much of a coincidence, which could mean only that this was the same girl ... the same bloody girl ...

The girl appeared again, the nightmares swirling behind her, the smile on her face as innocent as the blood-flecked grin on a lion after a kill.

The same girl, Alex was thinking, even though every sensible part of his being told him it couldn't be, but still ... and what if?

They were trapped, Alex knew it. Where they turned, this girl would follow. But he still had to try, so into first again and with a jolt he threw the car forwards, took a sudden right, kept accelerating, took a left, then saw sanctuary ahead: Imber church.

'We can't outrun her or it or whatever the hell that is,' Alex said and nodded towards the church.

'You can't be serious,' Rachel said.

'You want to stay in this tin can or go somewhere we have a chance of defending ourselves?'

Rachel laughed but the sound was devoid of all humour. 'Defend? With what? Are you mental?'

'It's a church,' Alex said. 'Perhaps we'll be safe there.' He didn't give Rachel a chance to answer, drove towards the church and skidded the car to a halt at the gate. Alex grabbed his crook and was out of the door and racing to the church door without a glance back. He could hear Rachel coming up behind him, her footfalls punctuated by swearing.

Alex got to the church door, heaved it open, waited for Rachel to charge through, the wrench in her hands, then slammed it shut behind her, dropping an iron bar across it from the inside. He then led Rachel through another door and into the main area of the church. Rachel dodged past him as he shut a second door.

Alex leant against the door, breath sharp in his throat, heart racing, adrenaline coursing through him, his senses on fire. Nothing in his training had prepared him for this, either as a soldier or a priest. He could carry out covert operations, survive alone in the wilderness to carry out a hit on a target, kill pretty much anyone with his bare hands if he had to. And he could tell of what faith was all about, why he believed in God, help people come through their own personal darkness. But this? Whatever this was, and whatever it was becoming, he didn't think there was a person on the planet who would be prepared for it.

'Alex ...'

The wood of the door was cool against Alex's forehead as he did his best to gather his thoughts. Though right then it felt like trying to herd cats.

'Alex ...?'

What the hell was going on? Why was he caught up in it? How could any of this be real? It couldn't be, could it? None of it was possible! It didn't make sense because there was no sense to any of it. If anything, it was Colonel Blake's fault. He should've just sent it up the chain of command and left it well alone. But instead, he'd called Rachel and then they'd come to visit him, dragged him back not only into a life he'd given up on – he couldn't be a soldier and a padre; it was impossible! – but into a realm of actual physical evil which even the Bible didn't describe! No, this was insanity at best, and Alex was going to just walk out of this church right now. Yes, that's what he was going to do. Because none of this was real and none of it was his or Rachel's problem anyway.

'ALEX!'

Rachel's voice forced Alex from his thoughts. 'What?'

Rachel's answer was to pull Alex away from the door and turn him around. And just when Alex thought he'd seen everything, Matt was there, waiting for them, ready to show them just a little bit more.

CHAPTER TWENTY-EIGHT

THE CHURCH WAS LIT BY CANDLES, DOZENS OF THEM, huge creamy white columns standing on pews, on the flagstone floor, in the pulpit, their heads lit with yellow flames which flickered in the drafts ghosting around the chancery. Alex saw the blood then, beneath their feet, sprayed across the floor. As he followed it, walking deeper into the church, he followed its trail up the wall and above them and to a picture unlike any work of art he had ever seen, surrounded by the same writing and symbols they had found at Matt and Becky's house.

Alex had seen Doom paintings before, even studied them for a paper during his training. But this was unlike any vision of Judgement Day he'd ever seen. This? Well, this was perverted. It was Judgement Day turned on its head then ripped apart by rusting hooks. The figure in the place of Christ at the centre was not a thing to offer hope and eternal life of happiness, but a creature of such creative evil Alex half expected it to step out of the painting, reach out for him, and disembowel him for fun. In fact, wasn't it reaching out for him now, its empty hands outstretched?

That was the look in its eyes, something that spoke of the joy of seeing other's pain, but more than that, Alex realised. It was a hunger, a yearning and thirst to have the freedom to do whatever it wanted, however it wanted, to who or whatever it wanted. They were the eyes of pure anarchy and they chilled Alex's blood to ice.

'Hello, Alex ...'

It was Matt's voice and yet not, Alex thought, sounding to him as though he was being called to from the bottom of a cold, damp well.

Alex didn't reply. His eyes were still on the Doom above him. So were Rachel's.

'It's ... it's horrible,' Rachel said, stepping away from the painting.

Alex moved his eyes from the creature in the centre and cast his gaze across the rest of the artwork, taking it all in, finding nowhere in his head that could hold onto it securely, as though his brain was refusing to accept what he was looking at and instead rejecting it. Then the images moved.

'That's impossible,' Rachel said. 'It's ... it's just a painting!'

Impossible didn't mean they weren't seeing what they were seeing, thought Alex, stepping back, putting more space between him and the image of that creature whose eyes were now following him.

'Don't look at it,' Alex said, as much to himself as to Rachel, as the picture came to life, and the blood on the floor, splattered across the walls, started to creep slowly towards it, feeding it.

Alex forced himself to turn away, took Rachel's right arm and helped her do the same.

'It's just an hallucination,' Alex said, working to make

Rachel keep a hold on her sanity. 'That's all it is, okay? An hallucination.'

Rachel said nothing, but her eyes, Alex could see, betrayed the horror deep inside.

Alex, with Rachel at his side, started to walk down the central church aisle, which took them down the nave and towards the chancel, beyond which was the sanctuary containing the altar. It was here Matt stood, Becky at his side, held tightly on his left side, his hand around her arm, pinching her flesh. The lights of the candles grew more fierce as the windows of the church fell to darkness despite a new day outside breaking its way to dawn. The air grew warm, not because of the candles, though Alex could feel the heat from them as they walked past, but because something was being laid over the church, something vast and thick and impenetrable.

At the step up into to the chancel from the nave, Alex stopped and he held Rachel back from moving on any further. He held his crook at his side, wondering if it would be enough to protect them, pretty sure it didn't have a chance, that they didn't have a chance.

'Matt,' Alex said. 'You need to let Becky go.'

Matt's face was calm, emotionless almost, but his eyes seemed dead, lifeless. Around him shadows danced and flickered, as though caught in a candle's glare, except that the movement had a purpose to it. As Alex stared, the shadows took form, twisting into each other, coming together, forming great limbs which twisted and spun in on each other, flicking up and down the walls of the church. At once they looked like the legs of a spider, scratching at the ancient brick work to pull it apart, then they were the tentacles of some unknown deep sea monstrosity, oozing out like a thousand and one squid spilling into the cool air from a crack in reality.

Alex stumbled back, away from what he was witnessing, doing everything he could to keep a grip on reality.

The shadows continued to shift and morph, reaching out for Alex, stretching out from the darkness brooding behind Matt.

'Let her go!' Alex said, forcing his voice out through a throat dry now with a fear that seemed almost brittle.

Then, to Alex's surprise, Matt released her.

The shadows stopped moving, dust in the air seemed for a moment frozen still, and Alex's ears popped as a pressure change thrust itself into the moment.

An odd, metallic laugh raked its way through the church but where it came from Alex couldn't tell.

Becky didn't move.

'Becky? It's Alex. You need to move towards me, okay?'

Becky didn't move. For a moment, Alex wasn't even sure that she was breathing.

'Becky?'

Matt said, 'Leave me,' and Becky took a step forwards, then another.

Before Alex could stop her, Rachel stepped forwards and grabbed Becky, pulling her away from Matt's side. Becky didn't struggle and she moved as though drugged.

Rachel for the briefest of moments looked relieved and Alex dared to think that they could get out of this, but then he saw a movement in the shadows behind her and that look of relief split in two as Rachel's face snapped from relief to shock and a small bead of blood appeared at the top of her forehead.

Alex reached out for Rachel, but he was dragged back, Matt's huge arms in a choke hold around his neck, not enough to cut the blood supply to his brain and knock him unconscious, but enough to have him unable to move, to help. Alex tried to swing his crook up into Matt's face, but Matt knocked it away with his free hand. A smell hit Alex then, one of roasting pork, and he saw that where Matt had touched the crook his skin was black and charred. Why had that happened? It reminded Alex of something, but what?

The bead of blood on Rachel's forehead traced a line down to the bridge of her nose, paused, then was forced onwards as Rachel shuddered. As the bead ran down her nose, another bead followed, then another, until it was a thin stream of red flowing freely into and over her open mouth, down her chin, to drip down and onto the floor.

Alex struggled, fought against Matt's strength, but it was hopeless. The man was a monster and there was something else behind his strength, because nothing Alex did would cause the grip to falter. He scraped his heels down Matt's shins, kicked into them, stamped on the man's feet and toes to crush them, punched him in the groin, grabbed his balls and wrenched them so hard he felt one of them tear, but all to no effect.

Becky moved then, turning to hold Rachel as her body started to violently shake, gripping her arms by her sides, forcing her to stay on her feet as Alex saw two small hands, two bare feet, appear, the hands clamped on Rachel's head, the fingers seeming to try and work their way inwards, the feet and legs hooked round from behind, climbing. Then the girl's face appeared over Rachel's left shoulder. 'Hello,' she said. 'Hungry?'

CHAPTER TWENTY-NINE

THE SOUND WHICH FOLLOWED THAT CHILD'S VOICE WAS a sharp intake of breath from Rachel, brutally cut off by a crack like a pistol going off. Helpless, bile rising to burn his throat, Alex watched as the girl's fingers wrenched Rachel's skull in two, her scalp prised apart with horrifying ease, pulling the woman's eyes in opposite directions with a spray of blood and brain. The girl, still clamped to Rachel's shuddering body, plunged her hands into the woman's head as though searching for something, then with a tug, out came her hands holding a small, glistening piece of flesh between her fingers.

The girl clambered down to the ground. Becky let go and Rachel's body dropped like liquid. Matt still held Alex tight as the girl approached, not walking but skipping, holding out the piece of dripping flesh in front of her.

'It's the pineal gland,' the girl said, sliding closer. 'Descartes was right, you know? This tiny thing holds your soul ...'

The girl cocked her head to one side, smiled, then

popped the mess pulled from Rachel's broken head into her mouth, and swallowed.

'Ooh, yummy!'

Alex retched and vomit spilled from his mouth and down his chin, covering Matt's arm.

'What do you want?' Alex said, wiping his mouth, his voice choked by Matt, the words burning his throat to get out. 'Who ... what are you?'

The girl didn't answer. Instead, she threw a glance at Becky, who turned, walked up to the altar, and returned with a silver cup and a silver plate.

'Who or what I am doesn't matter,' the girl said. 'Not to you. Not any more.'

Alex watched as Becky placed the plate on the floor at her feet then held the cup out in front of her, close to his own right hand. He went to pull away but the girl grabbed his wrist and held it with ease. There was a flash of metal, a sudden searing pain, and Alex looked down to see blood spilling from his wrist into the cup, heat rising from it in tendrils of steam. When the cup was full, Becky pulled it away and the girl reached out to touch the wound. As she did so, Alex sensed a warmth in his arm and found that the bleeding had stopped, the wound welded shut.

'Can't have you die quite yet, can we?' the girl said. 'There are a few things we need from you first.'

Becky placed the cup onto the floor and returned with the plate.

Alex saw the knife this time, held in the girl's left hand. As it came towards him, he struggled, but Matt trapped his arms to his side as the girl lifted up Alex's shirt and started to carve.

The pain took Alex to another place. He'd suffered fractures, been in fights, been stabbed, shot, but this? Being slowly carved up pulled him from his own body, away from the pain. He could still sense it, ripping its way through him, forcing him to scream, but it was as though he was merely observing.

Was this what it was like to die, he thought? Was that what was happening now? Some Hell-spawned creature or whatever it was taking his life? But why? What did it mean? Did it mean anything at all? Did it matter?

Something else pushed into Alex's mind, something pressing against his left arm. Why would that matter now? He was dying! Why should he care what was in his pocket? But this something he was sure was linked in some way to what had happened to Matt's arm when it touched his cast iron crook. But what was it? What the hell on earth was it?

Alex forced himself to focus, dug deep to that part of him which he kept hidden away, an animal part built of survival at all costs.

The horseshoe from Matt's house ...

Against the backdrop of blood and pain, Alex wriggled his hand into his pocket, found the horseshoe, clamped his fingers around it. In front of him, the girl was holding something up. What was it? It looked like a slice of pork loin. She dropped it onto the plate held by Becky who by now was kneeling on the floor.

The girl said, 'This was all about you, did you know that, Alex? Not Matt nor any of the others. Just you, right here, right now. With me. Funny that, isn't it?'

Alex was listening but his mind was on the horseshoe now in his hand. It, too, had burned Matt. He had no idea how or why, but right now he didn't care; it was a weapon and given the chance, he would use it.

'There are many of us, Alex, and we are all connected, laced together by threads only we can see. All of us looking, all of us connected. Perhaps threads isn't the right word. Arteries? Tentacles? Anyway, here you are and here we are. It's very metaphysical so you probably wouldn't understand. And it all started back when you met some little friends of ours a few years ago, remember?'

'The Order,' Alex said.

The girl skipped with joy.

'Yes! That was fun, wasn't it? You were a bit of a find to be honest.'

Alex remembered again Colonel Blake's story about what had happened to him in Kosovo, the girl.

'Which one are you?' he asked.

'Which one am I of what?' the girl said.

'You're a demon,' Alex said.

The girl laughed and the sound was of rocks tumbling and waves crashing.

'Let me guess,' the girl said, 'you think if you can name me you can control me, right? Read it in a little How-To guide for exorcism, given to all priests, did you?'

'Kosovo,' Alex said, remembering what the colonel had told them. 'You were seen in Kosovo.'

'I'm seen everywhere,' the girl said, her voice drifting off to another place, then dancing with a darker sound that vibrated with a deep, far off hum. 'We all are. Call me a demon if it makes you feel better. But it's a small word, you know.'

Alex was playing for time, trying to get his hands free.

'Why were you there? It's no coincidence, is it, that the colonel saw you there, and now here you are and ...'

'Nothing is a coincidence,' the girl said, as a smile cut her face with the cold efficiency of knife. 'You know that,

Alex. And that goes for what happened with your Colonel Blake.'

Alex choked on his own voice: he hadn't said the colonel's name.

'I used him and he served his part,' the girl said. 'Not that he'd know that.'

Now all Alex could think about was the twins alone with the colonel. His strength was fading, and he couldn't help wondering that if there was a God, and that if what he was facing right now was the very opposite of that, then now would be a very good time for that God to put in an appearance or at least give him some strength to do something, to fight.

'Anyway,' the girl said, 'as luck would have it, your friend Matt went and stumbled in on a very old friend of mine, someone who was very happy indeed to see him and to jump right in there and take up residence! Then all we had to do was to work together and bring you here. And, well, here we are!'

The girl moved then behind Becky who placed the cup and the plate onto the floor in front of her. She then wrapped her arms around Becky's neck in a hug. 'And here you are!' the girl said, 'so I hope you don't mind, but I'd like to be getting on with things now, okay?'

The snap of Becky's neck, as the girl gave the woman's head a vicious twist to the left, drove a spike of hot anger deep into Alex's head. With a roar pulled from his gut Alex heaved his hand from his pocket and brought it up hard into Matt's face. The big man took the full force of the horseshoe in Alex's hand, the metal crunching into his jaw. Suddenly released from the neck hold, Alex spun round and went in again hard and fast with the horseshoe, hammering it into the face of his old friend, who fell backwards, his face not just broken but suddenly on fire. Alex didn't stop the attack, grabbed the back of Matt's head and brought it down into his knee, once, twice, three times, then threw him skull first into a stone pillar. The impact sounded like a coconut hit with a cricket ball and Matt dropped to the ground, his head on fire, not moving.

'Well, I wasn't expecting that,' the girl said.

Alex turned to face her, anger burning his blood. His old friend was behind him and dead, of that he had no doubt, but now wasn't the time for sorrow. His years as a soldier had taught him how to switch that stuff off until the time was right. Though, if he was honest, he wasn't sure if there was every going to be a time from this point forward that would be right to deal with what was happening to him now.

'It's just you and me,' Alex said, reaching for his crook with his right hand, the horse shoe still clasped tight in his left.

The girl smiled. 'Is this where you say something heroic, like, 'Let's finish this?' She laughed then, the sound a discord that grated in Alex's ears. 'Or will you offer yourself as a sacrifice if I promise to leave?'

'If that's what it takes,' Alex said, his eyes drawn to Rachel's corpse, to the broken body of Becky.

'The problem,' the girl said, 'is that you are already the sacrifice, can't you see?' The girl crouched down and picked up the plate and the cup. 'If I'm honest, a lot of this isn't really necessary, but some of this even the ancient ones are unable to remember the reasons as to why, so we go along with it, you know?'

A clattering at the church door broke Alex's concentration but when he looked up in the hope of finding a rescue team racing in to help, all he saw instead was that far end of the church fade to grey then to darkness so thick it had a skin.

'You are who we have all been waiting for,' the girl said, walking away from Alex and towards the darkness, towards the Doom, the plate and cup held high. 'And as God gave Mary a son, so our own Gods have given us you. Aren't you lucky?'

Alex made to follow the girl only to find that he couldn't move, his feet held by Matt who stared up at him through a demolished face. Except it wasn't Matt anymore, was it, Alex thought, because Matt was dead? And it hadn't been Matt for a long time, not since what had happened in those caves. His old friend, Becky, Colonel Blake, they'd all been used by whatever evil was now before him to get him to where he was now. Rachel had just been caught up in it by accident, and she was dead, too.

The girl was facing away from Alex and standing beneath the Doom, the plate and cup held high. 'It's time!' she said, and giggled.

Alex took his shepherd's crook and with every remaining ounce of strength he had left hurled it towards the girl. Deep down he knew it was the last act of a desperate man, that there was no chance he would even come close to hitting the girl, never mind doing her any damage, but it was all he had left. None of this made any sense. All he knew was that he had been used, that his faith hadn't protected him, and that in a few seconds he would be dead.

The crook whistled though the air, drove itself into the back of the girl to explode from her chest and take her off her feet.

Stunned by either his sheer good luck or amazing accuracy, Alex sensed a slackening of Matt's grip on his ankles.

He took advantage of it immediately, yanking himself free and hoofing the soldier hard in the side of his head hard enough to collapse the skull.

Alex sprinted down the nave, the horseshoe in his hand. Ahead, the girl had sunk to her knees and was staring at the crook jutting from her chest, the wound burning, flames licking at her clothes.

'How ...' was all the girl could mutter.

Alex reached down and tugged the crook free then immediately swung it around and into her, like a golfer at his first tee, knocking her into the ground, her face connecting with a wet thwack.

The girl tried to rise, but Alex pinned her to the floor with his left foot. The wound in her back was burning freely now. She struggled again, so Alex just pressed harder, raising his crook for the killing blow. Then the struggling changed to a shaking and at first Alex thought it was death throws because the girl was moaning except it wasn't moaning, it was laughter and he breathed in to ready himself for the kill, when he realised that something was missing. 'The plate,' Alex said. 'The cup ...'

'Exactly!' the girl said, flipping over onto her back but without the strength to rise. 'There's nothing you can do! Nothing!'

Alex stepped back, looked around for the plate and cup. They were important, but why? And where the hell were they? They weren't on the ground, or on a pew. He hadn't knocked into them. So where ...

And then he saw them, in the Doom painting above his head, clutched in the hands of the creature at its very centre. A creature now staring at him with eyes of darkness on fire.

'You see?' the girl said. 'Christ had his own communion and now we have ours!'

'But why me?' Alex screamed, his eyes cutting from the painting to the girl and back again. 'What's so special about me? And why now?'

The painting was moving, Alex realised, the colours running into each other, twisting into shapes of every colour and none.

'You are an enigma,' the girl said, her torso now charred and black as the flames continued to burn, chasing their way down her arms and her legs. 'You call yourself a man of God yet so easily do you fall to violence. Why? Because that is what you are! And that is what we need! Chaos! Confusion!'

'Christ gave himself freely,' Alex said. 'Or have you forgotten I know a little theology myself? If what you're looking for is that, then you haven't got it. I'm no messiah.'

'Yes, we have,' the girl said, 'and you have no choice, Alex, because you are what you are!'

From around them the darkness swept in, arms reaching out from it, bodies tumbling forward, grabbing Alex, yanking away the shepherd's crook and the horseshoe. He recognised the faces in front of him; they were the horrors from the facility where Matt had been held. But now they were here and Alex knew all hope was lost.

'Whatever it is, I won't do it,' Alex said.

'You have no choice,' the girl said. 'All we need now is a little bit of your soul ...'

Alex tried to move but was stuck fast, his whole body wrapped in the things which had come after them only a couple of days ago and from which he and Rachel had only just escaped. Then a pain lanced its way through his body and he screamed, but the scream did nothing to help, as something scratched at his skull then rammed its way into it.

The last thing Alex saw, the last thing he felt, the last thing he believed and wished for and hoped, all of it was snuffed out as his own skull was torn in two.

Then nothing.

CHAPTER THIRTY

The church door burst inwards, splitting apart into a million splinters, flame and dust chasing them. Through the dust a man walked, and as he entered the church, he loaded another grenade into the launcher slung under the assault rifle, which was up and in his shoulder. He moved quickly, silently, efficiently, covering all possible points on the way where instinct told him something could by hiding, waiting to come out and attack him. But nothing did. The church was quiet and the morning was bleaching the windows with a sun as bright and as golden as he had ever seen. Which only made what he found before him all the more grotesque.

The church, even to the man's old, trained and experienced eye, was a lurid canvas of blood and horror. He wished he could say that he'd seen worse, but he couldn't. Bits of what he was now staring at were equal to other terrible things he had witnessed, but altogether as part of the same whole? No. Nothing came close.

How late he was to the party he wasn't sure, but that he was late at all was enough. He swore, spitting the words out on globs of phlegm that spun in the air to land amongst the awfulness. Taking his phone out, he started snapping photographs, gathering evidence, like he always did. And the stench! It burned the back of his throat, stung his eyes, was so thick before him that with every step more of it was kicked up to meet him. He knew it wasn't just the smell of death, but that something worse was mixed in with it, a rot of souls now leaking into the world from a place void of anything good. He quickly pulled from a jacket pocket a pot of menthol-scented grease and dabbed it under his nose. It was too late to be properly effective, but at least it did something to make the reek more bearable.

The man slipped further into the church and down the nave, but only as far as he needed to, stopping at the two bodies lying beside each other on the flagstone floor of the nave. Glancing further down the church, the man saw three further bodies, each broken and twisted, but they were just casualties of a war they wouldn't have even known was being fought.

Crouching down, the man looked closely at the two bodies in front of him. One was small, an older child or an adolescent he thought, but that was only a guess, the body being a blackened statue of smouldering charcoal. Beside it was the one he'd come for, who he'd hoped to help, but that he could see was now surely too late. He reached a hand to the smaller, blackened body and at his touch it crumbled to dust, rolling away on a squall of wind blowing in from the open door behind him.

It had taken him too long to piece the clues together. First had been the report of the discovery in the caves, a thing hidden for centuries which should have remained hidden. But it had escaped and hitched a ride back to England. The soldier who had unwittingly brought it back had seemed strangely okay after the incident, and the man had supposed that the thing which had been inside him had moved on in an attempt to stay hidden for a while. But he had been wrong and the thing had taken root and, if he was honest, could he have ever foreseen any of this? What a god-awful mess. The emails he thought would've been enough to get things moving in the right direction. He tells the colonel, the colonel tells the padre, the padre rescues his friend, and then he swoops in and makes the padre realise his true calling, that there was an organisation out there looking for someone with his particularly unique set of skills. Nice and easy, right?

Wrong.

Hideously sodding bastard wrong.

Because other things had been in play, hadn't they? And he'd been little more than a pawn in a game he had no idea he had been playing.

Raising his head, the man stared up at a blackened section of church wall above his head. He could make out scratches of paint at its edges, but nothing else to give away what had been here before, something else which had remained hidden for so long, even from him. He'd heard rumour of it, the Doom that would tear open a door between dimensions, rip a hole so deep that the planes of existence on either side of it would never be the same again.

Yes, thought the man, it was too late. What had been done had been done and he hadn't caught on quick enough to prevent it. He was an old fool, too old for this, too old for any of it. Retirement was calling him. He deserved it. A little shed on an allotment. Some homebrew. Falling asleep after an early afternoon ale. Yes, that, all of it.

God, he was tired. Right now, all he wanted to do was to walk away, find a quiet corner in an even quieter pub, and sink his sorrow into a few pints of ale. Would anyone really care if he did exactly that?

'Well?' the man asked out loud. 'Would you?'

No sound came, just a breath from the door, which brought in with it the rich smell of a new spring day, cutting through the stench of death that surrounded the man with an unexpectedly sweet scent.

'It's impossible,' the man said, as though caught suddenly in conversation with an invisible companion. 'I mean, just look at him!'

The man knelt down, resting a hand against the bloodied right cheek of the body in front of him.

'This is different,' the man said, never for once thinking how odd his one-sided conversation would seem if someone was listening in. 'Raising the dead is one thing, but this isn't just dead, it's a ruined husk! I'm no miracle worker! That was your job, remember? I know it's a long time ago, but time for you is irrelevant, isn't it?'

Another breath came through from the door, chased by bird song, which sang bright and joyful.

'I won't do it,' the man said. 'I can't! Too much has been taken already. And who's to say I can get enough back? What if I don't? What then? What if I just make things even worse?'

But as the words left his mouth, he was taking something from another pocket, a little zipped leather pouch. He opened it to reveal a small silver flask next to which lay a small silver lidded pot. From the pot he took a wafer and placed it on the tongue of the body in front of him. Then he pulled the stopper from the flask and upended it, wine flowing freely out, catching the wafer to take it down into the corpse's throat.

Nothing happened.

The man shook his head and sighed.

'See? What did I tell you?'

He stood up and turned to leave.

Breath came once more, only this time it wasn't from the door and it didn't carry with it a world waking to new day.

This breath, wrenched from an invisible split in the darkness and shadows that skulked in behind pillar and pew, came on the back of a scream, the primal and unearthly roar of a fractured soul called back from an eternal promise to wage war.

The man stood back and watched.

And prayed.

THE END.

GLOSSARY

ACOG – Advanced Combat Optical Gunsight providing up to 6x fixed power magnification, illuminated at night by an internal phosphor

AKs/AK47 – assault rifle, first developed in the USSR by Kalashnikov

AR-15 – lightweight semi-automatic rifle

Bergen – military style rucksack used by soldiers

Chatnet – closed channel on which soldiers communicate using PRRs (see below)

Chinook – helicopter, most often used for transporting equipment or troops

CO – commanding officer

CQC – close quarters combat

C8 Carbine – compact assault rifle, firing 5.56mm rounds, manufactured by Colt

D Notice – an official request to news editors not to publish/broadcast items on specified subjects for reasons of national security

Flashbang – non-lethal explosive device used to temporarily disorient an enemy's senses

Foxhound – Light Protected Patrol Vehicle used by British forces and replacement for the Land Rover Snatch

GCHQ – Government Communications Headquarters responsible for providing intelligence to the government and armed forces of the United Kingdom

Glock 17 – 17-round 9mm polymer-framed pistol

Helmet Cam – tactical camera worn on the helmet

IED – Improvised Explosive Device, which can be placed on or in the ground, used by suicide bombers, and sometimes activated by remote control

INT – intelligence

ISIL – terrorist militant group Islamic State of Iraq and the Levant

Laphroaig – one of the greatest single malts in the world

Medevac – emergency evacuation of a casualty from a war zone

MOD – Ministry of Defence

MTP – multi-terrain pattern camouflage printed on equipment issued to British forces

NVG – night-vision goggles

On point/point/point man – soldier at the head of a patrol

Padre – army chaplain

PRR – personal role radio: small transmitter-receiver radio allowing soldiers to communicate over short distances, and through buildings and walls

PTSD – Post Traumatic Stress Disorder

RPG – Rocket-Propelled Grenade

SA80 – semi-automatic rifle made by Heckler & Kock: the standard British Army rifle

SAS – Special Air Service: elite special forces unit of the British Army, founded in 1941

Scoff – food

Scrape – shallow area dug out of the ground to provide cover/shelter

Tail-end Charlie – solider at the rear of a patrol

The Regiment – other name for the SAS

Trooper – SAS soldier

UKSF – United Kingdom Special Forces

X-Ray – enemy combatant

ACKNOWLEDGMENTS

This book, and all the ones which will duly follow, has been a long time coming. Whether it's any good or not, well, that's up for you to decide. I'm not saying it's great literature, or expecting it to be, but I'm hoping it's a blast to read, and that you'll be willing to stick with me and Alex as we continue on with this adventure into darkness.

So, what about those folk who've got me back to the tippy-tappy sound of my keyboard? After all, you'll need someone other than me to blame, right? Well, it's a long list, and I'm not going to mention everyone here, because there are more books and more pages in which to give them their dues. But for now ...

First shout goes to Jake West, film director, blonde god, lover of the weird and the wonderful, and a man who, with a phone call out of nowhere, and a friendship I treasure, was integral to Padre becoming real in the first place. He also gave me my big-screen moment, interviewing me as part of the bonus features in a Hellraiser boxset! He gets first dibs on the film rights and a massive hug next time I see him.

Ryan Oliva deserves a mention, and not just for scaring the hell out of me in The Seasoning House. He was the inspiration behind the character of Matt, though possibly more terrifying.

Lucy Clements gets a nod as well, seeing as she made me realise I needed a strong female in the story and thus Rachel Coates was born.

Then there's everyone from the Author Collective and Tommy's Lair, who have supported and encouraged and insulted me through all of my forays into writing. Without whom ...

Emma, my two boys, my family: here, words fail me.

And finally, to you, the reader. Thank you for taking a punt on this little book. I hope you enjoyed most of it enough to tell others and can forgive the bits that you didn't just enough to read on.

ABOUT DAVID J. GATWARD

David J. Gatward was brought up in the church, had his first book published when he was 18, and has written extensively for children and young adults. He has held numerous roles in the publishing and writing industry, including as a ghost-writer and researcher specialising in the military and extreme sports, and worked with thriller writer and former SAS soldier, Andy McNab. He has also seen a number of ghosts. Padre is his first work of adult fiction.

For more information:
www.davidjgatward.com
info@davidjgatward.com

Printed in Great Britain
by Amazon

41044455R00132